Will Travel for Love

Sweet Nothings Bake Shop, Book 2

Kristen Dixon

THIGPEN-
GANDY
PUBLISHING

THIGPEN-GANDY PUBLISHING

Contents

ONE

Agent for Love

My life's work was basically helping people in love go places. Sure, that sounded
fun enough. You know what wasn't fun? Sending people on amazing honeymoons day after
day . . . fifteen-year-anniversary trips to Rome,
eighty-year-olds renewing their vows in Thailand
. . . while you had nobody to even go home to at
night, except your dog, Barc. Barc was awesome. I
mean, how could he not be? When your name was
Barcelona, you were bound to be pretty great. But,
puppy snuggles could only take you so far in life, and
I couldn't shake the feeling that I was missing out on
more.

The afternoon was dragging by. If I didn't know better, I'd say my clock was broken. But, the real source of the time suck was the extraordinarily unhappy trio of siblings sitting across the desk from me, who'd been bickering non-stop for the last fifty-four minutes. *Fifty. Four. Minutes.* I counted.

"No, I am not paying extra so Mom and Dad can go ride around on a boat and not snorkel. That's absurd," Tom, the eldest, protested.

"What's absurd, Tom," Trina sniped, "is that all you care about is penny pinching when this is our parents' fortieth anniversary! For Pete's sake, they put up with you thirty-seven of those years—we should be buying them a medal instead of a snorkeling trip."

Teresa, the youngest, sighed. That's pretty much all she'd done for the last—oh!—fifty-*six* minutes, now.

"Now you listen here, Trina—" Tom started again, but I cut him off before World War Three could get underway.

"Okay, guys. Let's take snorkeling off the table for now. I have an alternate suggestion! How about a glass-bottomed boat? It's serene, it's scenic, and nobody has to get their hair wet. It's pretty much the ideal activity, given that your mom doesn't want to snorkel," I suggested, trying to keep my tone sweet and supportive as I slid three copies of a glossy brochure across the desk.

"Now, that could work!" Trina said thoughtfully.

Tom snorted in derision. "Sure, that's what you say about everything. Let's blow more of Tom's money!" His anger was a palpable presence in the travel office at this point.

"Daphne, thank you so much for your time today. We'll discuss things on our own and make a few decisions before we make a follow-up appointment to book." Teresa shocked me by finally speaking as she stood and tapped the brochure against her palm.

"Of course." I shot to my feet as well. "That sounds great. If you have any questions at all, you have my email address."

Despite our politely efficient exchange, Tom and Trina were still tearing into each other, unmoved by our cues.

"You ought to know what a big deal it is that they've been married forty years, Tom, given that no woman's ever been able to put up with you for more than three! Remember Celeste, Teresa? She didn't even last four *months*!"

The happy jingle of the bell over the front door pulled all of our gazes as my next appointment walked in, and—thank the good Lord—stopped Tom from snapping back at his sister.

He shoved his chair back so forcefully as he stood that it wobbled for a moment before settling back to the plush peach rug. Without another word, he turned on his heel and stalked off, leaving his younger sisters behind as he brushed past a stunned Marlie and Tucker, who were waiting right inside the door.

Teresa shot me one last apologetic look before tugging a fuming Trina out the door.

"Come on in, y'all, don't be shy. How are you this afternoon?" I put on my best chipper voice for my long-time friend, but it was feeling a bit thin as she and her fiancé settled into the newly vacated chairs.

Marlie perched on the edge of the chair, but leaned in and asked, "Are you all right? They seemed upset. Shouldn't people be happy when they're in a travel agent's office?"

I just shook my head. "Yeah, they are having some trouble deciding on the details of a surprise vacation. It's a challenge with three very different people planning a single trip. We'll get there eventually." I drummed my fingers on my desk for a moment, trying to refocus. "Okay, so, today we're going to be talking about something *much* more fun. Did you guys decide if you wanted to go hot or cold for the honeymoon?"

Tucker gave me a lazy grin. "Yes, ma'am, we're going hot."

I rubbed my hands together with glee. "That's what I was hoping you were going to say! Okay, I have two amazing options for you. If you'll turn your chairs towards the wall here, I've got some pictures to show you!"

I hit a few keys on my computer, and the wall-mounted big-screen lit up with lush rainforest surrounding a waterfall pouring into an amazing turquoise pool.

The next forty-five minutes were spent with me showing off extravagant Costa Rican adventures, followed by the relaxed island luxuries of Jamaica to the sounds of their oohs and ahs.

When I was done, they both turned back towards me with lightly glazed expressions. "Daphne, that was even better than I'd hoped! And those options are both in our budget?"

"They sure are. The Jamaican resort is all-inclusive and a surprisingly good value, and the exchange rates are particularly good for both destinations. So, do you want to think about it, or do you want to go ahead and get it booked?"

The glance they shared was overflowing with excitement, and after a moment, Tucker nodded. "Let's book it. Which one, Marlie? Jamaica or Costa Rica? You pick and I'll pay."

"Phew, Marlie! You got you a good one, girl. Don't make him say that twice." I shot her a supportive smile.

She twirled a strand of auburn hair around her finger and furrowed her eyebrows, taking the decision seriously. "Well, Costa Rica looked beautiful, but after all the stress of wedding planning, I think I'd really want somewhere relaxing, more so than adventurous. If that's okay with you, Tucker? That zipline over the waterfall thing looked spectacular."

"Marlie Abernathy, how many times do I have to tell you—there's no scenery on God's green earth that compares with the beauty right in front of me. All I care about on our honeymoon is the woman with me on the trip."

Marlie looked down with a small smile and blushed to the roots of her hair. "Tucker, I don't know what to say."

My usual saleswomanship deserted me for a brief second, as my heart bled watching their tender moment. *What I wouldn't give for a man to look at me like that.* The thought brought me low, but I pushed through for the sake of my friend, and my job.

"Well, now, it sounds like you two are going to Jamaica!" I pasted a smile on for my dear friend, refusing to let my loneliness poison their moment in the sun. Marlie was as sweet as a Georgia peach, and Tucker was a true gentleman. There wasn't a couple on the planet more deserving, and I was determined to do my part to make things special for them, even if I was dying on the inside. Besides, Marlie was a year older than me, and she was only now finding the one. Didn't that mean there was hope for me, too?

"I guess we are," Marlie said with excitement.

After the happy couple were all booked and on their way, I put up the "Be Back in Thirty" sign, and headed down the sidewalk towards the Sweet Nothings Bake Shop. My best friend in the whole entire world, Bea, worked there—and when life gets you down, there's nothing to pick you up quite like your best friend, and a fresh apple donut. The bakery was my go-to for both.

The day was beautiful, but uneventful as I strolled down the street. The normal, light afternoon traffic drifted by, leaving me to an island of my own thoughts. And lately, they'd been pre-occupied almost constantly with Jasper Lewis. Ever since I'd met him at my brother's game night a month before, I'd been a woman obsessed.

It was understandable, really. I was in the travel business, where at least seventy-five percent of my clients came in to book travel for either honeymoons, or anniversaries. Both great occasions, neither of which pertained to me and my perma-solo status. And, dang it, but I was a perfectly successful, single adult—I had a job, a little house of my own, Barc, my awesome best-fur-friend—but, something was missing. And Jasper, with his crisp British accent and his five o'clock shadow captured my interest like no other man in town had in years.

Normally, I was no shrinking flower about going after someone that interested me, but I'd been hemming and hawing about taking the initiative with Jasper. He wasn't someone I could see myself getting bored with—even from the first time we met—and that scared me.

As my brain continued the fruitless Jasper-loop for the nine thousandth time, I arrived at the bakery. When I pulled open the door, the smell of fresh-baked heaven slapped me right upside the head.

Hearing the door chime, Bea pushed her way out of the swinging doors from the kitchen while drying her hands on a towel and spotted me. She grinned as I approached the pristine glass display cases. "Daph! I'm so glad you're here. I have a fresh batch of donuts which I need your expert opinion on. Are you willing to try a cinnamon chocolate today, instead of your usual apple?"

I threw my hand to my chest as if mortally offended. "Excuse me, did you really suggest I *skip* an apple donut, as if that is an option? How long have we been friends, Bea?"

She threw her hands up in exasperated surrender to my undying love of apple donuts.

"But I'll take both. You know, you really have to compare and contrast for a true evaluation, anyways."

She quirked a smile at my response. "I knew you were the woman for the job! Grab the corner table, and I'll be there in a jiffy. Celia won't mind manning the counter for a bit."

I couldn't help but smile at my bestie, always experimenting to make things a tiny bit better. Her boss and the owner of the shop, Celia Ann Montgomery, encouraged her to follow her baking muse, and the bakery, which had always been a town staple, was thriving with the two of them working together.

I strolled over to our usual corner, and pulled out the little pink gingham-clad pouf seat facing the window. The sidewalk was empty at the moment, but that never lasted long, and I loved people watching. Something about the endless possibilities of each person's day fascinated me.

I bobbed one foot impatiently and stared out the window until Bea arrived, three donuts in tow.

"Okay, so, this is my newest creation. I know it sounds weird, chocolate and cinnamon. But . . . the cinnamon dough is just so good, it seems like a crime to only serve it in the fall, you know? So, I was trying to think of a way to bring it into every-day-awesome status, and well, I dipped it in chocolate, and sprinkled it with a sugar-and-spice streusel."

Her explanation of the finer details went in one ear and out the other, as I picked it up and took a bite. "Wow, this is good. Like *really* good," I said around my second mouthful of donut bliss.

She clapped and asked, "You like it? But, on a scale of one to ten, how much do you think it compares to the plain chocolate one?"

I waved my hand for a minute. "Eleven. This needs to go on the menu."

"Yes! I thought so, but you know I'm biased." She picked up her cinnamon chocolate confection, and we both fell silent for a moment as we enjoyed our treats. I caught a hint of movement in my peripheral vision, and turned to see who was passing by . . . then froze, my mouthful of donut divinity forgotten in an instant.

There at the corner, crossing the street—and heading this direction—were none other than Jasper Lewis—object of my personal obsession—and my brother George.

"What is it?" Bea asked, noticing my sudden stillness. "Oh, it's George!" She hopped up excitedly to meet him at the door.

They'd been dating a few weeks now, and were about as happy as I'd ever seen a new couple. We'd all grown up together, and once they'd finally admitted their mutual attraction, they'd gone together like honey butter and a warm biscuit. Watching them click had only served to underscore my blatant lack of romantic prospects.

Bea, despite all her delightful qualities, didn't have a handsome brother waiting in the wings for me to fall madly in love with. *Rude*.

The moment George walked in, Bea gave him a quick peck on the cheek, and grabbed him by the hand to pull him to the counter and the waiting tray of fresh donuts. Her cheerful unveiling of deep-fried deliciousness across the room washed over me without impact, because my eyes were only interested in the tall, dimpled Englishman who casually shut the front door in their wake. So self-assured, he slid one hand into his slacks pocket and then surveyed the bakery's interior with slow interest.

When his eyes landed on mine, where I sat tucked away in the corner, a smile lifted one corner of his lips. To my surprise, instead of trailing after George to the counter, he crossed and greeted me.

"Daphne! It's lovely to see you today. How have you been?"

My brain—usually so quick with a fun quip—froze up like a 1997 desktop computer; it was busy panicking about the possibility of a chocolate mustache. In the end I blurted, "Great! Just, ahh, eating donuts and booking honeymoons," and waved my half-eaten donut at him, like a loon.

Smooth, Daphne, really smooth!

He lifted one dark eyebrow at me. "Well, that *is* an interesting combination. Do you have a recommendation—on the donuts, or destinations?"

I was saved from another embarrassing response by Bea and George's approach.

"Oh, Daphne is a travel *whiz*!" Bea bragged as she took her seat again next to me. "If you ever get the chance to go on a trip she's booked, you'll be amazed! We did a girls' weekend last year, and every minute detail was perfect."

"Well, I'll keep that in mind. I don't have anything planned at the moment, but maybe I should change that," he said with a twinkle in his eye.

"Do you two want to join us? We're always up for handsome company such as yourselves." Bea gave George a shy smile with the last bit.

He sighed. "I'd love to, but unfortunately we're heading to a job site that's having issues. Jasper was a good sport about stopping by so I could sneak a quick visit on the way."

Her face fell. "Oh, okay. Well, I'm glad we got to see you for a minute, at least."

He gave her a hug, and then turned to me and wrapped me in a brief embrace as well.

"I know, I'm sorry to have to drop by and run. We're trying to make the best use of Jasper's time before he moves on to the next job. This guy is a genius," he said, clapping Jasper on the shoulder with enthusiasm.

Jasper waved a hand in dismissal before settling it onto the leather bag strap slung across his shoulder. "I'm doing my job, nothing special."

You are so, so wrong about that.

With that thought banging around like bongo drums in my head, they said their goodbyes and walked right back out the door.

TWO

Have Your Cake . . .

T he door closed behind them with a muted thud, and I forced myself to look down at my donuts, rather than follow them down the street with longing puppy dog eyes like I wanted. I had my pride, after all. Bea seemed deflated, too, so we sat in silence for a moment, fidgeting with the donuts we'd been so excited for a short time before.

Our malaise was interrupted by the sound of a dainty chair scraping across the burnished wood floors of the bakery. Celia plopped down in it, and fanned her gorgeous face with one hand while the other brandished one of Bea's new creations, less one bite.

"Now, I've already had a bite of this delicious confection, so I know that's not what's got you two down. What are two young, flawless beauties such as yourselves looking so glum about? Is it the gentlemen that just made their exits?" Celia prodded.

When neither of us answered fast enough to suit her, she continued with a warning tone, "Well, if you won't tell me, I'll have to call their mamas." She punctuated her threat with another bite, and an accompanying Southern lady staredown. You'll know when you see it—it's the one that makes little boys with muddy knees straighten up and say, "Yes, ma'am."

Bea chuckled at Celia's stern inflection. "No, Celia, don't call Mrs. Anderson—and, do you even know Jasper's mom? How would you call her?" She paused thoughtfully. "Anyways, everything's fine. I'm bummed that George had to go straight back to work, that's all. I don't know what's wrong with Daphne." She eyed me thoughtfully, as if just noticing my sullen expression herself.

Celia scoffed, "What am I, an amateur? There is not a mother on this *planet* I couldn't get in touch with if their son was misbehaving, believe you me! Now, more to the point—did he break off plans with you to go back to work? You're still scheduled for another two hours, I thought." She flicked her wrist up to check her diamond-encrusted Cartier watch.

"Oh, no. I wasn't expecting him at all—it was a surprise visit." She looked down at her lap, and a small smile crept onto her face. "He said he was thinking of me, and couldn't go another minute without seeing me."

"I'll be. Then why are you looking down? When I was your age, I'd have been over the moon if a man was whispering sweet nothings like that in my ear."

I gave Celia a look out of the corner of my eye and asked gently, "Only at our age? No interest anymore, Celia?"

She gave me a sad smile. "Oh, no Daphne. My Richard . . . well, he and I had the real thing. Life-long, til-death-do-us-part, Johnny Cash-and-June Carter love. Once you've had that, there's no settling for second rate, no matter how pretty a masculine package it comes wrapped up in." She paused, lost in his memory for a moment before she shook it off. "Speaking of pretty packages, that Jasper might not be from these parts, but he'd *sure* look handsome in a white suit under a wisteria-blossom wedding arch come spring. Don't you think, Daphne?"

To my eternal mortification, I blushed to the roots of my hair, and for the second time today, my brain went utterly blank.

"Ahh, I see," Celia said, taking in my tomato-red cheeks. "I've always appreciated redheads. Beautiful, and easy to read as the Sunday paper. You girls have a good chat, now. I'm going to work on the croissants for tomorrow." She paused before pushing through the swinging doors. "Bea, we're going to put these donuts on special for Friday. They're divine, as usual!" Then she walked back into the kitchen, the doors flapping in her wake adding to her flourish.

I turned to Bea, only to see her staring straight at me with her mouth hanging open.

"You are going to catch flies like that."

"Excuse me, but if I'm not mistaken you have it *bad* for Jasper. Why didn't you say anything?" she asked, breezing straight past my fly comment.

I shrugged one shoulder, and looked out the window to avoid the question.

"Come on, Daph—you can tell me anything. Why the secrecy?" she queried more gently this time.

I gave her a pointed look, but there was no real heat in my words. "You're one to talk. How long were you in love with my brother without a peep to me?"

She had the good grace to look abashed at the dig, but didn't back down. "You're right, I kept things hidden for a long time, and for what? You and I are still best friends, and now I have George in my life as more than I ever dreamed was possible. So, spill. You like Jasper?"

With a sigh, I let the words slip out in a hushed voice. "I do. I find him fascinating, and gorgeous, and brilliant."

She clapped in excitement, and leaned in to squeeze my arm. "That's amazing, Daphne! I could totally see you two together. I mean, he's brilliant, you're brilliant. He's tall, and has that dimple thing going on. You are like a porcelain doll. Oh, you'd make beautiful babies. Your mom will be *thrilled* about that." Bea chuckled.

I shook my head. "No, Bea, there aren't going to be any beautiful porcelain dimple babies, okay? This is why I didn't say anything. You're excited, and I want to go crawl into a cave for a month." I dropped my head into my hands.

"What? Why? Did he turn you down or something?" She sounded ticked off. Goodness, I loved my bestie. She had my back no matter what.

"No, he has no idea I'm into him, and that's the way it's going to stay. It would never work out, Bea."

"Why the heck not? He's single—I already asked George," she proclaimed.

My head shot up from my hands of its own accord. "Why in the world would you do that?" I asked in mortified horror.

She shrugged, as if it was nothing. *This is not nothing, dang it, Bea!*

"I could tell you were intrigued the night we met him at George's, so I asked him. It's not a big deal. For all George knows, I'm trying to set him up with somebody else. He literally didn't even ask why I wanted to know."

Thank God for small blessings in the form of male indifference. "Fine, but, please—don't make a big thing out of this. He's not sticking around, and that's that. There's no point in pursuing something that can't go anywhere."

The corner of her mouth quirked up with skepticism. "Really, now? It couldn't go, say, to dinner? Or, oh—I know! A nice movie, an evening stroll by the river—those all seem like pretty excellent places for it to go."

I sighed in defeat. "Bea, sure, it would be great to go on a nice date. But I like him too much to keep it light and then watch him leave. I know myself, Bea, and I'd be torn up for longer than it would last to begin with. I just . . . can't. Not at this stage of my life. I mean, every flippin' day, I watch couple after couple come in, and I book them some fantastic trip to celebrate their happiness and love. Dang it, Bea. I want a relationship worth booking plane tickets for! Not some short walk by a muddy river. I don't think that's too much to ask—I'm almost *thirty*."

Bea snorted a laugh at my dramatics. "Yep, you're practically a dried-up old spinster at twenty-six. I'll alert the town newspaper. Mr. Sanderson will be thrilled since last month's headliner was about the higher than average number of Georgia hoppers." She shook her head, and then her voice dropped to a softer tone. "Daphne, you are going to find the right guy. But if you keep cutting them off, how will you know if it *could* go further? You might get hurt—that's always a risk—but you might get surprised in a good way, instead. If you feel that strongly about him, it sounds like he's *worth* taking the leap for."

"I know, Bea. But with Jasper it feels too real. And, yes, I realize that sounds entirely ridiculous. We've had barely a few polite interactions. But, I'm so drawn to him, I already don't want him to leave. I mean, right now at least there's a chance I'll bump into him on the street. But once he goes on to the next job, that's it. Door—*slam*." I clapped my hands together to accentuate the point.

"Daphne, I really don't think—" Bea started, but was abruptly cut off by the front door flying open, and an incensed Dolly Blake stormed through.

"Oh, this is going to be good," I muttered under my breath, grateful for the distraction.

"Celia! Celia Anne Montgomery, where are you?" the woman hollered, barely within acceptable indoor volume limits. Her chest was heaving from the speed at which she'd steamrolled through the door, causing her floral taffeta blouse to quiver indignantly.

Bea instinctively leaned closer to me and clutched my arm, eyes wide at the spectacle.

Celia pushed through the swinging kitchen doors, unhurried, with a triangle of croissant dough in hand. "I'm right here, Dolly. My lanta, what are you caterwauling about? Is somebody dead?"

She huffed indignantly. "May as well be! Do you know what they've done to Jude's? Have you heard?!" Her voice rose a full octave by the time she spoke the last word.

"Jude's Restaurant? No . . ." Celia trailed off. She didn't ask, but with Dolly, you didn't ever need to. Wait two seconds, and she'd fill the silence like a waterfall would fill a puddle.

"They put in one of those tea *machines*. Can you believe that? A machine! Like sweet tea is just some soda you can spit out of a little canister." She fanned her red face. "I never thought I'd see the day!"

Celia continued rolling the triangle of dough, but her brow furrowed at this news. "Well, I admit I'm surprised, but everyone tries something new now and again. Have you tried the tea it makes?"

Dolly slapped her hand down on the counter. "Tried it? I would not *subject* my taste buds to that abomination in a tea glass! We have got to do something about this." She wagged an exaggerated finger in Celia's direction. "This is how it starts! Somebody changes a good Southern thing for a cheaper substitute, and next thing you know all the houses are shoddy and the drug dealers move in down Main Street! Well, not on my watch! I will *not* allow it!"

I glanced at Bea—we were both on the edges of our seats, captivated by the small-town drama that inevitably followed Dolly as closely as her perpetual cloud of Beautiful Magnolia perfume.

"Now, Dolly, I can see you are already riled about this, but I'm telling you—Beau and Janie Jude aren't going to do anything that hurts business. If the tea machine is unpopular, they'll be brewing it up again like Granny did in no time. There's no need to go off ruffling feathers."

She gave a haughty sniff. "Well, if you won't take this seriously, I will take it seriously enough for the both of us! You just wait and see." With that, she turned on her nude wedge sandal, and stormed out with the same bluster she'd stormed in with not five minutes ago.

Celia shook her head, shot the two of us an amused look, and wandered back into the kitchen with her perfectly shaped croissant.

My phone's alam startled me out of the drama-induced stupor.

"Shoot! I've got to run, my next appointment will be at the office in five minutes. Thanks for the donuts!" I said, as I grabbed my remaining treats and jogged out the door.

"Fine, but we're not done discussing Jasper!" Bea lobbed the words at my retreating back.

Dang bestie is a pit bull in a pink apron. Once she gets after something, no way is she letting me slide.

THREE

Thoroughly Mixed

I had nothing to wear. Officially, thoroughly, nothing worth writing home about to wear to this mixer. Rather than continue staring fruitlessly at my tired closet, I flopped backwards onto my bed with a huff, arms and legs spread-eagled as I stared at the ceiling fan. Its lazy circles didn't inspire me to go back to the closet and continue the search. Instead, I grabbed my phone and texted Bea.

Daph: *Nothing to wear to this mixer. *Fork Emoji, Eyeball Emoji**

Bea: *You have more clothes than anyone I know. You're being too picky. It's the monthly church singles mixer, not the opera.*

Daph: Nonetheless, my closet is mocking me. I don't even want to go, since you're not coming. But if I don't go, I'll never hear the end of it from my mom.

Bea: We always loved the monthly mixer! It will be F-U-N!

Daph: Hardly. We had fun because it was basically BFF night but with people watching.

Bea: Want us to come? You know we will. I've got your back, Jill.

Daph: Who's Jill?

I was distracted from Bea's messages by a cold nose pressing into my thigh. It was Barc, looking for an ear scratch. I reached down and gave my sweet beagle a good rub. "Who's a good boy? Barc's a good boy, that's right." The phone in my hand buzzed again, drawing my attention back to Bea.

*Bea: You know, 'I've got your back, Jack.' But you're a girl, so . . . Jill. *Thumbs up emoji**

*Daph: You're the best weirdo I know. But, thanks, I'm good. I have to get used to going solo at some point before you and my brother ride off into the sunset without me. *Barf emoji**

Bea: Never. You're totally coming into the sunset with us. Bring sunscreen.

Bea always knew how to put a smile on my face. Now I only had to keep it there for the next . . . two hours and forty-seven minutes. Barf. I gave Barc one last ear fondle and then heaved myself from my cozy bed to face reality.

I fidgeted with the hem of my bright yellow wrap dress as I sat in my truck in the church parking lot trying to convince myself to go into the fellowship hall.

"Well, Bert, I think this is it. This is rock bottom," I said, talking aloud to my trusty baby blue Chevy step-side. "I can't sit here all night, but I don't want to go in there, either." I abandoned my hem in favor of dropping my forehead to the steering wheel in dejection. "Why does being single have to be so hard, Bert? Why can't we just be born with some sort of indicator stamped on us with the name of our other half, like a sci-fi movie. That would be awesome. No muss, no fuss. No *mixing*."

Bert was a good truck, but unfortunately even if he had the answers, he wasn't able to share them with me. So after a few more moments of silence, I dragged myself off of his cozy bench seat & tried to look happy as I walked into the fellowship hall of the small church.

As I slipped through the door, upbeat music washed over me, followed closely by the smell of chili. *Ahh, it's cooking-contest night. Lovely.* Before I made it two steps into the room, I was swarmed by a few familiar faces.

"Daphne! Looking good, girl! Love the dress." Stacy reached out and wrapped me in a hug, which I returned. "No Bea tonight, huh?" she said, voicing dropping into a pitying tone.

"It must be so hard watching your best friend and your brother get together after all these years," Denise added from my right. The part she left unsaid hung in the air, waiting to be acknowledged. *While you're still single, sucker!*

I called upon my inner zen and reminded myself that politeness was next to godliness—or so my mother insisted—before answering, "Oh, now. I'm happy for Bea and George. They're perfect for each other, and it was about time the two of them realized it."

Denise slapped a dramatic hand on my arm, which she probably meant to be comforting. It wasn't. "That's so gracious of you. You're such a loyal sister."

I could feel my zen slipping away faster than a greased pig, and I hadn't been here five whole minutes yet. I was saved from an answer by loud clapping coming from the serving area.

"Hey, y'all, I'm so glad you all made time in your busy schedules to be here with us tonight!" Missy Sumner clapped with enthusiasm, encouraging us all to join in as she beamed around the room. "Anywho, tonight is the quarterly singles cook-off, and boy does everything look scrumptious! This month, the theme was Hot Chili and Cool Cakes, so I'm sure you'll be delighted with all the offerings. Don't forget to grab your voter card near the silverware, so you can vote for your top three favorites in both categories! Now, Assistant Pastor Lee, would you pray for us?" She bowed her blonde head without waiting for his response, and the rest of us followed suit.

Pastor Lee's voice boomed throughout the room with a prayer of thanks, and then everyone queued up to sample all of the contest dishes. I put myself at the back of the line, as frankly I was in no mood tonight to try chili ten ways. I was still a few people away from the first pot of brown mush when a low voice next to my ear made me jump.

"Is this some sort of American mating ritual, where singles are forced to show off their cookery skills before they're allowed to marry?" I spun half way to take in Jasper—the owner of the most delicious accent in town—standing right behind me.

"Jasper! What are you doing here? I mean . . . Hello, it's nice to see you, but, uhh, I wasn't expecting you this evening."

He cocked a half-grin. "Well, I wasn't expecting to be here either. I dropped back by the bakery today for an afternoon cuppa and Celia told me this was 'the place to be' tonight."

That was not the answer I was expecting . . .

"Really? She said 'the place to be?' Huh. Well, I don't know if I'd go as far as all that," I disagreed.

"No? You're here, so it can't be all that bad." He gave me a wide, genuine smile, and it was like the sun breaking through on a foggy morning. My heart sped in my chest, and I felt my body sway towards his without permission from my brain.

"That's true, I am here . . . but mostly for my mom's sake."

He tossed his head back and laughed. "Your mum? Has she got big plans for marrying you off, then? Is there a list I need to be on for her consideration?" He bumped my shoulder lightly with his, and I blushed furiously.

"No, no list."

"That you know of." He gave me a rakish smile, which I couldn't help but return despite my embarrassment at the topic.

"What can I say, she really wants grandkids. She thinks George and I are holding out on her on purpose, at this point."

"Are you?"

I smacked his arm lightly before answering, "No, I am not, thank you very much! Just haven't found the right person. What's your excuse?"

He shrugged. "No excuse. It's difficult making a real, lasting connection when you're never in one place for long."

My stomach knotted at the reminder that his time here was temporary. "I bet that is difficult."

"You get used to it after a while, but lately, I've been wanting a change." His intense gaze bored into me and made my knees melt.

"Oh, really? Change can be a good thing," I murmured, lost in his deep brown eyes.

He leaned in closer, and I swayed in too, as if we were magnets drawing each other in. A throat clearing behind us pulled me from the moment, and I remembered our surroundings in a rush.

Mark Bradenton, a friend from high school, was right behind us in line. "The line's moved," he said with a sheepish expression before quickly looking away.

"Sorry, mate," Jasper said. "After you, Daphne." He gestured towards the now completely open space in front of us.

I hurried forward, grabbing up a bowl and spoon, and spotted a chili pot midway down that was still nearly full. I ladled several scoops into my bowl. After I found empty space at a table, I set everything down and spun to go grab a glass of tea, and nearly wiped out Jasper and his bowl of chili. He stepped back smoothly, raising his bowl and avoiding the collision.

"Excuse me, miss, but I think your blinker's out," he said, all smug humor.

My hand flew to my burning cheek of its own accord. "I'm so sorry! I was going to get a drink, I didn't realize you were right behind me. Can I get you something to drink, too?"

"Sure, whatever you're having is fine." His grin could be weaponized. That five o'clock shadow with that dimple in his chin would knock women out en masse.

"Okay," I said and rushed away from the scene of the near miss. *Get it together, Daphne. You can talk to the man without being a spaz!*

I forced myself to take a few inconspicuous deep breaths, and fixed two glasses of sweet iced tea. Once they were ready, I turned and calmly walked back to the table, and noticed that Mark and Missy had joined us, too. I set the glass in front of Jasper, and then sat down at my place to his right without a word.

He looked over and gave me a warm smile, and my stomach did a flip that I was already starting to associate with being in his presence. I returned a small smile, and then focused on my chili. Missy, thankfully, was carrying the conversation like a one-woman hostess machine.

"So, Jasper," she drawled, "tell us, what is England like? I've always wanted to visit London." Her voice was sweet as honey, and her eyes lingered on Jasper like he was the biscuit she was looking for.

"Oh, it's lovely. London is the city that never sleeps, and it's never dull. The area where my parents live is a bit more rural, however, and has more rolling pastures than city skyline."

"It sounds delightful."

"Thank you. I do miss it at times. But the States have quite a bit to recommend them, as well." He looked sideways at me and picked up his glass. He didn't look down, just took a sip, and then the strangest look crossed his face.

"Uh, you okay, Jasper?" I asked, as he seemed to be choking.

With a grimace, he choked down his mouthful of tea and spoke—"What *is* that? Gah, that's horrendous." He picked up the glass and inspected the unassuming contents.

I couldn't hold back a giggle at his expression. "You've been here over a month—haven't you tried sweet tea yet?"

His eyebrows shot up his forehead before he shot back, "This is simply *not* tea. It bears no resemblance to tea—it's pure sugar."

Mark laughed at his sour expression and chimed in—"It's an acquired taste for outsiders."

"Must be, but I confess, I don't particularly want to acquire a taste for that." He shook his head again.

Missy's laugh was a dainty tinkle floating through the fellowship hall. She put a hand on his arm, "Oh, Jasper, you are so refreshing. I could get used to having you around."

Jealousy I had no right to flooded me at the innocent contact, and my stomach turned for a whole different reason. To distract myself, I picked up my spoon and scooped up a large bite of chili. I chewed and started to swallow, when the heat washed over me like a tidal wave of pure hellfire. The burning first started on the back of my tongue. Then, my eyes began to water, and my lips felt like they'd been dipped in acid. My eyes cast around for a napkin so that I could wipe my mouth, but I'd forgotten to grab one.

My frantic search finally turned up a napkin, on the far side of Jasper's food. In too much pain to ask, I leaned over and snatched it up, and furiously wiped my burning lips. The sting abated slightly, and I grabbed my glass of tea and chugged. By the time it was empty, it no longer felt like my mouth would be a suitable playground for hellhounds.

"Are you okay?" Mark asked, staring wide-eyed at my unladylike behavior.

Jasper didn't comment, simply slid his glass of tea over to me, and unobtrusively pushed his own bowl of chili away.

"Peachy," I croaked out, my throat still angry from the assault.

"You've got to be careful with Stacy's chili. She calls it five-alarm for a reason. Not everyone can handle the heat, it seems." Missy's poor attempt at hiding her smirk only ticked me off, but she didn't stick around long enough for me to retort.

She sashayed over to the table by the desserts, flipping her blond locks over her shoulder as she went. With a staccato clap, she drew everyone's attention. "Okay, y'all, now that the chili portion of the evening is pretty well wrapped up"—she looked at me with raised eyebrows before continuing—"it's time to move on to the sweeter side of things. Dessert cakes! Now, if any of you ladies would like to slice your cakes for serving, come on up!"

There was a smattering of applause from around the room, and several women bustled up to fiddle with their cakes before serving.

Jasper leaned in with a conspiratorial gleam in his eyes. "Did you make a cake? Do you have something you need to go faff about with over there?"

I shook my head. "No, Bea's the baker in our lives. My specialty is eating what she makes and giving her feedback. For instance, she once decided to leave the eggs out of her cookie recipe, because she wanted to see if she could. It was my job to taste test them, and tell her to go put the eggs back in."

He smirked. "Ahh, yes, a *very* prestigious occupation. I can see why you need to reserve your talents for the tasting side of things. Maybe one of these days I'll make something for you, so you can put your skills to good use."

I leaned forward, once again drawn into his gravitational pull. "Oh, so you're a baker?" I put a little skepticism in my voice, just to see how he'd react.

He didn't rise to the bait. "Oh, not much of a baker. But I'm an excellent cook. I'd love to have you—"

I held my breath, pretty sure he was about to invite me over to dinner, when an unusual crackling, snapping sound cut him off mid-sentence.

"What in the dickens?" I muttered, and Jasper also whipped his head around, looking for the source of the sound.

The next thing we saw was a bright, flashing light from one of the cakes. Missy jumped back, batting at her hair with a look of horror on her face.

"Are those . . . sparklers?" Mark asked from across the table, where I'd completely forgotten he was sitting, wrapped up in Jasper as I had been.

"If so, those are some *huge*-behind sparklers," I commented drily.

The crackling continued for another moment, and then a single, tiny tendril of smoke trailed its way lazily up from the white linen tablecloth the cakes were sitting on. In a split second, an ear-piercing alarm filled the room. "Fire. Fire. Please walk to the nearest exit. Fire. Fire. Please walk to the nearest exit."

Next up were the flashing lights, and then, from above us, a strange popping sound echoed down the length of the fellowship hall. I looked up. "What the—"

I was interrupted from that thought by water. *It's raining, indoors? No—fire sprinklers!*

My shock turned to disbelief as what felt like buckets of cold water doused us all. Feminine screams mixed with the fire alarm, and I just blinked for a moment before Jasper grabbed my arm.

"Come on, Daphne, let's get out of here!"

My feet finally caught onto the idea that staying meant getting wetter, so up and off we went towards the back exit of the fellowship hall.

Jasper held my hand as we jogged out and didn't let go as we descended the steps to the parking lot. Once the ceiling was no longer raining on us, we both stopped, chests heaving.

"That is absolutely not what I anticipated tonight! You Southerners sure know how to make things interesting; I'll give you that." He let out a shocked bark of a laugh and ran his hand through his soaked hair. In the fading light, it looked dark and thick.

I reached up and shoved my own sopping, bedraggled locks back from my face before I answered, "Oh yeah, really interesting. I think we could do with a little *less* interest next time." The hair clung to my hands, the side of my face, and my neck in what I could feel was a damp bird's nest. *I must look terrible.*

Flashing red lights and sirens pulled our attention towards the parking lot, as the county firemen arrived to handle the disaster inside.

"Well, we should probably both head home and get cleaned up. Can I walk you to your car?" Jasper asked, polite despite the soaking.

"You really don't have to!" I protested.

"I insist. Come on, we're probably parked near each other, regardless." He offered his elbow as if we weren't dripping wet and ridiculous, and I couldn't help but appreciate his positive attitude. Many men would be ticked off that their evening had been ruined, but he kept his chin up and went on calmly. No anger, no fuss, no complaints about soaked shoes. I slipped my hand into the crook of his elbow and couldn't help but notice the warm strength radiating through beneath his drenched button up shirt.

A shirt which I now noticed was clinging enticingly to a well-defined chest, and tapered waist. It was dark enough I couldn't make out any details, but I felt a warm flush heat my cheeks regardless. *He really is handsome. And polite. And perfect.*

The sounds of our shoes squelching as we crossed the parking lot broke through my enamored musings. Thankfully, Bert wasn't far.

"There's my truck—thanks for walking me." As we reached the tailgate, I stopped walking and faced him, reluctantly pulling my hand away from his firm bicep. He gave me a warm smile, and I felt it to the tips of my toes.

Then, to my surprise, he reached forward with one hand, as if to cup my cheek. I held my breath, anticipating the touch. At the last moment, however, he swiped with his thumb under my eyelid before resting his hand against the side of my face.

What is he doing? I was confused for a few seconds, and then it clicked. Mascara. Buckets of water. Raccoon eyes. Mortification filled me, but before I got too far down my mental path of horror and embarrassment, his words stopped me in my tracks.

"Still every bit as beautiful as the first time that I saw you. Drive safely, Daphne. I hope to see you again soon." He leaned forward, and I was frozen in place as he drew near. *Is he about to kiss me?*

A few short inches were all that remained between us when someone called me from across the parking lot, "Daphne, hey!"

An out-of-breath and sopping wet Mark Bradenton jogged up to us. Jasper pulled back, and I thought I saw the briefest moment of disappointment cross his face, but he buried it quickly.

"Hey, Mark. Everything okay?" I asked, hearing the breathlessness in my own voice at what almost—maybe?—happened.

"Oh, yeah! What a crazy night, huh?"

"Uhm, yeah. Crazy, for sure." I gave him a small smile to be polite, but my eyes were like magnets drawn over to where Jasper waited, hands tucked into the front pockets of his slacks.

"Definitely. I always thought Americans' love of fireworks was overemphasized. Apparently, some of the hype is true." He punctuated that observation with a wink, and my knees turned to butter. *Get a grip, Daph!*

Mark laughed and slapped him on the back. "You're not wrong, man, some things definitely live up to their reputations around here." He turned and fixed a smile on me at the same time Jasper did, and a lump rose in my throat as I fought the urge to fidget under their combined scrutiny.

There was a long pause, and Mark finally said, "Well, I'm going to see if they need any help with cleanup, I just wanted to catch you before you left." He leaned over and gave me a quick hug before striding back across the lot.

"He's a nice chap," Jasper said idly.

"Yes, the nicest," I agreed, mind racing a mile a minute as silence descended again. *Is he going to try to kiss me again? Was that even what he was going to do, or did I just imagine it? Be cool, be cool!*

He gave me another knee-melting smile. "Have a good evening, Daphne."

"You too, Jasper." The words came out quieter than I intended, but he acknowledged them with a dip of his chin before strolling across the lane to a black two-seater sports car.

I watched him go, until I saw him stop at the door and turn. He gave me a wave, and then stopped. After a moment, I realized he was waiting for me to climb into the truck. Embarrassed all over again, I quickly climbed into Bert's bench seat, still dripping, and cranked him up.

"That is not what I expected tonight, Bert. Not what I expected at all," I muttered to the faithful old truck as I carefully backed out of the space. He didn't answer, but his engine purred a touch louder than usual, almost as if he approved of the upheaval.

Sparklers, sprinklers, and firemen paled in comparison to the fireworks I felt with Jasper.

FOUR

Winner, Winner

Today was going to be a busy one—I had back-to-back appointments at the agency pretty much non-stop after nine a.m.—but hopefully I'd finally be able to snag a quick catch-up with Bea on all that had gone down at the singles mixer. Three days was far too long to go without dissecting things with my bestie, and I hadn't seen Jasper since, which had me feeling all sorts of confused. I parked at the agency, dropped off my bag inside, then hoofed it towards the bakery as quickly as I could while braiding my hair over one shoulder. I was more than ready to get myself a donut to bolster me for the long day ahead, and hear what she thought about the near-kiss with a handsome British man.

Already picturing that sweet, fried goodness—and much needed perspective from Bea—I rounded the corner and almost ran smack into a line of people.

What in the world? What is everyone waiting for? Rather than stop to ask, I hurriedly went around and towards the front door of Sweet Nothings, and saw to my dismay, that's where the line was headed. Luckily, Bea was just outside the door, order pad and pencil in hand.

"Bea! What's going on?" I called as I approached, and she gave me a quick wave and a shrug before returning her attention to cotton-topped Mrs. Lindy, who was ordering.

"Now, let's see . . . What do you have that's not too sweet? I'm getting old, you see, and I don't need all that sugar you young things seem to favor," Mrs. Lindy said in a chastising tone.

"If you want something savory, you would probably enjoy a croissant, or maybe a gruyere quiche."

"Gruyere? What in the Sam Hill is gruyere? It sounds like gray hair, and I sure hope Celia's not baking *that* up these days." She patted her fluffy white hair with righteous vigor.

Bea chuckled. "No, Mrs. Lindy. It's a type of cheese . . ."

"Hey, Daphne!"

My attention was pulled towards the line of waiting guests, where I spotted Mark Bradenton. "Hey, Mark." I walked over towards him, mentally cursing the delay. "What's everyone doing waiting out here?"

"You must not have seen the paper yet today," he said matter-of-factly.

"No, why?" I asked.

He pulled the folded paper out from under his arm, flattened it out, and passed it to me. The bold headline made my jaw drop.

"Shut the front door. Are they serious? Boycott Jude's, over *tea*?"

"Oh, they're serious, all right. Dolly wants that tea machine out, and she wants it out yesterday. She went to the paper, the church bulletin, and the mayor's office before the day was out."

"Huh . . . well, Dolly is rather determined." I looked down at my watch. 8:57. "Shoot! I don't have time to wait. I'll have to come back later. Bye, Mark!" I passed his paper over and headed back to the travel agency at a brisk jog, my strawberry blonde braid flapping in the wind behind me.

Business had been positively booming lately. I don't know what was in the water, but spring in Adele Georgia was the peak season for travel bookings. I was so slammed that not once did I have time to check my email all day. After eating the now soggy sandwich I'd packed at home this morning in the five minutes between my one and two o'clock appointments, I actually had ten whole minutes before my next appointment was due to come in. I'd just opened my inbox to see if anything needed my attention, when the over-the-door bell chimed, early.

Stifling an inward groan, I ignored the brimming mailbox and turned to greet my prompt two o'clock, Susan and Louis Daniels.

"Daphne, I'm sorry we're early. We are so excited. I mean, Europe! Who wouldn't be excited?" Susan Daniels clutched her tan leather purse under her arm tightly, whole body wound up at the possibility of a great vacation. How could I begrudge them? I couldn't.

"Come on in, guys. There's nothing I'd rather do than get you all set up for Europe. Now, have you had a chance to look over the brochures I sent home with you last time? And go over the emailed links?"

Louis Daniels snorted, before answering, "Oh, I don't know, only about a hundred times in a week, wouldn't you say, dear?"

Susan looked unabashed at the call-out and was still sitting on the edge of her seat. "He is acting tough, Daphne, but he's looked them over with me at least half of those times!"

Louis smiled fondly at his wife, and scooted his chair a bit closer to put his arm around her.

"Hey, you can't be too sure. So, since you've looked it all over, which of the three routes do you want to go with?"

"Paris," she said with a dreamy sigh. "Definitely Paris." She looked over at Louis like he was the most handsome man in all the world. He nodded his assent.

"All right, then. Let's get this trip rolling, shall we?"

Their enthusiastic nods were all I needed to get back to business.

By the time five o'clock rolled around, I was dead on my feet. I finally had the time to glance at my inbox, but no energy whatsoever. Most of it seemed to be just resort promotions, which I got every day by the droves. There was one email labeled "Important!" from the franchise office, so I set a reminder to check it out first thing tomorrow morning, and logged off for the evening.

As I was locking up for the evening, my cell phone buzzed and flashed that I had a message from Bea.

Bea: Dinner tonight? Sushi? Jude's?

I thought about the paper this morning, and gritted my teeth before responding.

Daph: Jude's. 7?

Bea: *Thumbs up emoji*

That settled, I drove Bert home to my tiny yellow house on the outskirts of town, and was greeted by a euphoric Barc.

"Hey, Barc! Hey, sweet boy. Did you miss me? I missed you, with your handsome face and your little waggy tail. Let's go outside, come on." He skidded around so fast his tail whumped against the wall as he ran for the back door, and I shook my head at his antics.

My initial lack of energy evaporated that quickly, getting that friendly greeting from my loveable dog. As I let him out and watched him tear across the backyard, nose to the ground, I couldn't help but smile. I left him to his backyard adventures and turned to kick off my shoes back by the front door. I'd put them away later. Then I wandered into the kitchen and grabbed a tiny powdered sugar Donette out of the bag on the counter. Bea would be appalled at my pre-bagged snack, but I had next to no cooking skills, and I wasn't that picky.

The thought sucked me back to the night before, and the conversation with Jasper. He didn't seem put off that I couldn't cook, at least. Most of the men around here expected a potential wife to be able to whip up a casserole at fifty paces with a blindfold on. I could maybe whip some cling film off a microwave meal, if it didn't require scissors.

We all had strengths, and mine weren't the kitchen—such is life. I preferred to define myself with all the things that were great about my life. Barc. My little sunshine house, which I was proud to have purchased on my own. My awesome job. Bea, the best bestie ever. George, when he wasn't being too George. My parents, who still doted like I was five and reciting the alphabet, no matter what I achieved. Bert, for sure.

I had a good life so far, and I was dang proud of all I'd accomplished on my own. *But something is still missing.*

I wandered on slow speed into my bedroom to pick something different to wear for dinner, since I'd dropped mayo on my shirt at lunch. Through the open door to the bathroom, I spotted my yellow dress, still hung over the shower curtain rod to dry from last night's fiasco, and my cheeks heated in embarrassment. The almost-kiss alone was enough to make me blush, but when I'd walked through the door and seen that my nice, modest dress when dry, was *completely* see-through once it had been soaked by the fire sprinklers, I'd been appalled. The horror of realizing Jasper had walked me to the truck that way had been followed quickly by appreciation that he'd been a perfect gentleman. Thinking back, his eyes had never once strayed from my face, and he hadn't said a word—probably trying to save me the embarrassment.

I pulled on a solid black tee shirt, my favorite pair of broken-in jeans, and dug out my nice black wedge sandals. Cute, yet supremely comfortable. After letting Barc back in, five minutes of ear scratches, and refilling his bowl, I hopped in Bert's cab and headed back towards town to Jude's. Riding along on a spring evening like this, with the windows down and country music turned up on the radio was about as good as it got. No worries—just the hot sun, the blowing breeze, and my own thoughts.

The moment didn't last long. My phone started ringing from my purse on the seat next to me, so I quickly grabbed it and put it to my ear.

"Hello?"

"Ms. Anderson! Hello, this is Imogen from the main office. How are you this evening?"

I stifled my sigh, and did my best to sound pleasant when I answered, even though I was about worked out, and it never boded well when the agency's corporate office called me during off hours. "I'm great, Imogen. How is everything there?"

"Oh, they're wonderful, Daphne. In fact, I was calling to follow up with you on our email earlier today! Are you excited?"

"Uh, well, about that . . . it has been very busy so I haven't had time to read it. I can assure you that whatever you need, I'll get it to you tomorrow morning, first thing." *Even if I have to get to work half an hour early and have a caffeine IV put in to do it.*

"Oh, no! I am sure you have been busy, and that's quite all right. I guess I'll deliver the good news directly, and save you the email."

Thank heavens.

"All right, I am pleased to inform you that you are the top agent in your entire district for the quarter, and as a result you've won an all-inclusive trip for four to any of our top ten destinations! Congratulations, Daphne, you are doing so well, and we are so pleased to be able to celebrate your achievements. If you have any questions, let me know. But, I'll let you get back to your evening now, ta-ta!"

With a click, the line went dead, but I continued holding the phone to my ear in shock for another belated moment before dropping it back to the seat.

"Well, hot dang, Bert! Did you hear that? I won a free trip!" I reached over and smacked the dashboard affectionately. For the first time in days, I had a smile on my face.

I got front-row parking at Jude's restaurant, and walked in the front door with a major spring in my step. Bea was going to be so excited when I told her about the trip; I felt all bubbly just thinking about it. As I breezed in, I stopped in my tracks at the sight before me. Jude's, as the favorite town dinner spot, was usually bustling even on a mid-week night. Tonight, it was dead as doornails. So dead, in fact, that the place was completely empty, except for me—a state I had never once experienced in my entire lifetime of eating here. The scene sent me from jubilant to ticked in five seconds flat, which made me even madder since my good mood had been soured by the crappy situation.

Voices from the back drew my attention, so I strode that way to let them know they had one customer, at least. Before I rounded the corner to the kitchen, however, Janie Jude and Celia came out, chatting.

"Celia, I don't know for the life of me what to do. We've never had a lull like this, not since the day we converted the old tack shop to a restaurant and opened. We can't go on like this forever, and frankly, this whole mess is upsetting. How could the whole town turn on us over one small change?" Janie confided in Celia.

I cleared my throat so as not to eavesdrop, and gave them both a friendly wave before closing the distance.

Celia nodded in my direction, but addressed Janie with her arm around the other woman's shoulders. "Janie, this whole thing is being blown out of proportion. People won't last long with this ridiculous temper tantrum—they'll realize Dolly's led them all astray yet *again* with her hysterics and before you know it, this place will be bustling like usual. Although I truly didn't think she had *this* much influence." Celia's deep frown said it all as her eyes skipped over all the empty tables.

Janie shook her head, expression morose.

"It's a crock of bull, if you ask me!" I chimed in, adding one more supportive voice to the mix. "Everybody in this town loves Jude's and we'd all be up the creek if y'all closed your doors. Dolly's going to run herself out of steam, and then this will be over and done with. Adele, Georgia isn't Adele, Georgia without Jude's, and that's all there is to it."

I heard the front door swing open, and turned to see Bea walking in while brushing flour out of her long black ponytail. "Hey, y'all. How is—Whoa, where *is* everybody?"

Janie let out a dejected sigh before answering, "Hello, darlin'. Looks like you three lovely ladies are my only customers tonight. Sit wherever you'd like, and I'll grab the menus."

Bea shook her head and looked angrily at Celia. "Celia, this is not right! How can everyone just boycott Jude's over tea? I mean, their tea is delicious, but, come on! We change our menu all the time, and nobody bats an eye."

Celia looked thoughtful for a moment and tapped her chin. "I don't know, I'm flummoxed myself. Somehow, we will figure this thing out."

Bea and I picked the big corner booth—because why not?—and Celia wandered over to stand next to Janie behind the hostess station. The phone rang, and she picked it up and seemed to be writing down an order.

"So, how was the rest of your day? You never made it back to the bakery for your afternoon pick-me-up," Bea observed, drawing my attention back to our table.

"It was crazy. Actually, it got crazier on the way here. You'll never guess! I got a call from the agency management—"

Bea groaned. "Ugh, those are never good. What now?"

I couldn't help but chuckle at her reaction, as she knew my past woes like they were her own. "I thought the same thing, but actually, apparently I am the best performer this quarter in the whole district, and I won a trip!"

She slapped the table in her excitement. "Nuh-uh! Really? That's great, Daphne! You've been working your tail off, and you deserve some relaxation time. Ugh, I'm jealous. All this mess means we're slammed, too." She gestured at the deserted restaurant tables surrounding us. "We actually had to run out before noon to buy more butter, as we went through a week's supply in the last twenty-four hours."

"Well, it turns out you're in luck, too, because I won a trip for *four*, and it wouldn't be the same without you. Can you come? We have a month to pick the locale and go."

She clapped her hands together, and practically levitated in her excitement. "Are you *serious*?! Of course I'll come! Where are we going?" The glee on her features brightened my mood again, and I quickly laid out our options and a few highlights of each. Janie came and went taking our orders, and we never stopped debating the benefits of Grand Cayman vs. Mazatlan vs. bundling up and seeing the sights in Alaska.

It felt like no time had passed at all and we'd narrowed it down to a warm-weather destination as Janie slid our plates of steaming hot dinner in front of us. "Personally, I'd pick Grand Cayman. Beau and I went there on that cruise you helped us with for our twenty-fifth a few years back, remember? Anyways, the people were friendly, and the water was gorgeous—the most amazing turquoise I'd ever seen in real life. If I was going to stay somewhere for a few days, that's where I'd go!"

Bea nodded, and tucked into her plate of pot roast as Janie walked back to the hostess stand to continue shooting the breeze with Celia, as the two of them sipped iced teas.

I picked up my cheeseburger with both hands, and took a giant bite. Juice dribbled down my chin in a most unladylike fashion, but there was no one here to see, so I wasn't too concerned. Bea was used to my barbarian eating habits from childhood. After we'd both made some progress on our dinners, Bea finally asked, "So, if we go, and George is the third person, who is going to take the fourth spot?"

I sighed, and set my delightful burger back on the plate. "I don't know! We need someone who'll be fun to travel with, and I think it should be a guy, so George has someone to do dude stuff with when we're at the spa."

"Excellent point. Do you want to let him invite a friend? I'm sure he knows somebody willing to room with him for a few days to enjoy a free beach vacation." She gestured with her fork, and a piece of pot roast wobbled precariously on the end as she spoke.

"Ehh, I love my brother and all, but he's like a golden retriever sometimes. He's friends with literally everyone. Take Finn, for example—that man is the laziest human on the planet, and somehow George is still friends with him. *Lives* with him." I shuddered at the thought of Finn as a roommate. "So, he needs some guidance on who to pick."

Bea laughed. "He's not that bad, Daphne, he's friendly! It's a good quality."

"Yeah, says you, who's all moon-eyed any time he's within fifty feet. Nope, we will be suggesting someone. Since he is so friendly, he won't care who we pick," I pointed out.

She acquiesced with a shrug. "That's true, he probably won't care. But that still leaves us without a fourth person." She punctuated the statement by pointing her collard greens at me, and squinting one eye.

"Don't remind me," I muttered right as the front door opened again. Bea and I both whipped around to see who else was breaking the Tea-Gate boycott, and spotted Jasper walking in with his hands in his pockets.

My perpetual case of butterflies took wing the instant I saw him. *Hello, handsome.*

FIVE

Duck, Duck, Goose

T he sight of him sent a frisson of electricity through me, and I felt myself leaning towards him without a thought. *Girl, you are pitiful. Settle down! He hasn't even noticed you're here, and you're practically drooling.*

Bea cast a sidelong glance at me, gauging my reaction. I did my best to keep my face neutral, but no way was she convinced. *I'm going to hear about this later.*

He spoke quietly to Janie and nodded at Celia, who pointed him in our direction. He turned, and waved as soon as he spotted us, a smile lighting up his face.

"He looks happy to see youuuuu," Bea said in a sing-song voice.

"Bea, shut it!" I whisper-yelled as he approached.

"Jasper! So nice to see you. Do you want to join us?" Bea invited him, an evil glint in her eyes directed at me.

"Oh, well, I would love to, but I couldn't possibly interrupt girls' night. George has informed me that those are sacred," he said in a serious tone. "Also, something about it being a condition of being allowed to date his sister's best friend." His gaze flickered back and forth between me and Bea, as if trying to gauge both of our openness to him staying.

Bea gestured magnanimously towards my side of the large corner booth we occupied. "Jasper, that's very sweet of you—and George—but we don't mind the occasional party crasher. Right, Daphne? The more, the merrier!"

I am going to strangle her for this! I finally found my tongue again, and spoke up. "Of course, Jasper, sit down!" A moment later, I realized he was expecting to sit on my side of the booth, and slid over.

"Well, I do hate to bring a lovely conversation to a halt, so don't stop on my account."

"Oh, well—" I started, but didn't make it far before another voice cut in.

"Jasper, you might be just the solution to the girls' little problem!" Celia's voice was sweet as molasses, and drawled out equally slow. "You see, Daphne here—shining star that she is"—Celia waved to me with a proud smile—"has outperformed every other regional travel agent this quarter. Can you believe that?"

I blushed furiously and picked at the corner of the napkin in my lap, hoping that if I simply pretended this wasn't happening, no one would notice me sitting there. Jasper's warm tone made me look up, and we locked eyes as he spoke.

"I most certainly can. She is brilliant in every possible way."

I sucked in a breath, and stared deeply into his hazel eyes, as if I were a snake and he was a charmer playing one of those lute things. Flute? Lute? Either way, I was toast. So distracted, in fact, I almost didn't catch what Celia said next.

"Well, that trip she won is a trip for four. The girls were just trying to decide who should be George's roommate for the weekend, and I think it should be you." Her matter-of-fact pronouncement snapped me out of my stupor, and I jerked around as if I could silence her with my mind, but she continued, ignoring my wide eyes and hanging jaw.

"It seems like a perfect fit. You four are already acquainted, and it would give you a chance to get to know each other better. What do you say, Jasper?"

Jasper vacillated under Celia's sharp gaze. Her words might have been slow; however, her mind was anything but. Sharp as a tack, she could make a pastor squirm like a schoolboy. "That is a lovely idea, but I couldn't impose. I'm sure George has someone he'd like to bring along. In fact, his roommate—"

Celia scoffed, and put her hand on Jasper's arm. "Jasper, honey, you don't know this yet but Daphne's not letting Finn within a hundred yards of her vacation. No, they're in a real pickle, and it would be a cryin' shame to let a ticket go to waste. Right, Bea?"

I silently pleaded with Bea to read my mind and not go there. *Come on, Bea. Don't agree. I can't take four days in close proximity to him; I'll be head over heels.*

Bea looked back at Celia, and with a one-shouldered shrug, shattered my childhood hopes that the two of us would one day develop ESP. "I'm down. I'm sure George will be fine with it. Really, it's up to Daphne, since it's her trip."

As one, the three of them all looked in my direction, and I felt the tension of the moment building like a parade driving down my spine. "Uh . . . sure. Jasper, why don't you come with us?"

A slow smile spread across his handsome face, and my eyes lingered on the line of his strong jaw under that five o'clock shadow. Mouth suddenly dry, I was fully invested in his response.

If he says yes, I'm in trouble. But if he says no, I'll be crushed.

"I would love to. Name the time and place. I hear your trip-planning skills are excellent."

Celia clapped with joy. "I just knew it! You four are going to have a delightful time. I can't wait to see the pictures." With that, she wandered off, leaving the three of us to ourselves.

Once I relaxed, dinner with Jasper and Bea felt easy as breathing. That scared me more than anything, because if I was honest with myself, he felt like someone I could wrap myself in, disappear into. But I wouldn't want that, I was too independent. I took care of my own self, my own life path. I didn't want to be one of those girls swept off her feet—when I eventually settled down, I wanted it to be with someone who I'd walk side by side through life with, not be carried like a fainting princess.

As the last crumbs were pushed around our plates, Jasper laughed at something Bea said, and the throaty chuckle etched another crack into the protective walls I'd built around my heart. I caught him glancing at me out of his peripheral vision, and it hit me in that instant that maybe this wasn't a one-way street. Maybe he was interested in me, too . . .

" . . . Yeah, Jasper, you should have seen Daphne as a teenager. Woo! She was wild as all get out, and she knew exactly what she wanted. Actually, there was one summer in particular you'd have been interested in; you see, I was half in love with George even then, and after some serious arm-twisting I convinced Daphne—"

"Don't you dare finish that sentence, Bea! That was nearly a decade ago—he does not need to hear it." I cut her off swiftly, not wanting to relive the dubious glories of our red polka-dotted swimsuit summer.

"Daphne, since when are you such a buzzkill? Also, I don't know if you remember this, but a few short weeks ago you were all for torturing me . . . which is why I must tell you, Jasper, that we bought red polka-dot bikinis, convinced they'd have all the boys falling at our feet."

"Really, now? And how did that go?" He leaned in with an amused tilt to his head.

I cut in dryly, "Oh, plenty of them fell, all right. I knocked a few down myself for getting the wrong idea."

His eyebrows shot up, but I was genuinely surprised by the next words out of his mouth. "Well, good for you. No matter what you're wearing, a man should never press an unwanted advance on a woman."

"Amen!" Bea agreed, and leaned back against the booth cushions to rub her full belly.

Good gracious, every interaction with this man drew me in further. *Couldn't he have something imperfect about him? Give a girl a chance, at least.*

Realizing that both Bea and Jasper were staring at me, unable to hear my mental commentary, I felt the need to blurt something. Anything.

"I still have that bikini, in a box at the back of my closet." The instant it was out, I regretted it.

"Reeeeally, now," Bea's face transformed from my sweet, cheerful bestie to wicked intent in no time flat. "I guess you'll have to bring it on this vacation. I'm sure it still fits." The twinkle in her eye made me want to strangle her, but I forced myself to stay polite, noting Jasper's interest in our exchange out of the corner of my eye.

"Bea, we've grown and matured far too much for those suits. We're adults now, it's time to *move on*," I gritted out through my teeth.

"That's one way to go, sure. But another is more of the, 'If you've got it, flaunt it' variety. Show of hands, who wants Daphne to bring the bikini?" Bea asked, and I very deliberately folded my arms across my chest as she waved a hand in the air like some ridiculous three-year-old.

"Bea, don't be ridiculous. It's only the three of us, and no way am I voting for that. Plus, Jasper's not going to—" My jaw hung slack in shock, as I turned to the man himself for backup, only to find him waving his hand in the air, as well. "What in the blue blazes are you two trying to do, kill me?" I narrowed my eyes at Jasper accusingly. "Shouldn't you be on *my* side here?"

His grin turned devious, and his voice dropped to a lower register that made my palms sweat as he leaned in, and spoke quietly, "Sorry, Daph—I'm on my own side on this one. That bikini sounds *delightful*."

The brush of his breath, light on my cheek as he said *delightful*, sent heat blossoming down my neck like a tidal wave. Mesmerized, I heard myself respond far too breathlessly, "I guess so."

This time his smile was warm and slow. Meant only for me.

Too slowly, my brain clicked into gear again and I realized that I'd been snake-charmed into agreeing to wear a very revealing—and likely too small—bathing suit. *Not so fast, folks.*

"That is, on one condition . . . Bea has to wear hers, too." I arched my eyebrow in an unspoken challenge. What's good for the goose, Bea . . ."

She squinted at me, but gave a tiny nod of acknowledgement that I'd backed her right into the corner along with me. "Fine, if you insist. I'm willing to self-sacrifice for the greater good." She glanced quickly to Jasper and back to me, wordlessly telling me, in that way best friends do, that she was hell-bent on hooking me up with Jasper, by whatever means necessary.

At that moment, her phone rang, diffusing the tension.

"George, hi!" Bea said as she answered, excitement at hearing his voice after a long day snapping her right out of our silly dares.

I stamped down the envy that tried to rush in at the sight of my glowing best friend. I refused to let our friendship and her happiness be soured by my singleness.

A sigh escaped my lips, despite my resolve, and I turned back to my near-empty plate and picked up a fry. I swirled it aimlessly in the little pot of ketchup, needing something to do with my hands to distract myself from the conflicting emotions.

Jasper's deep, accented voice caused me to freeze mid-twirl. "Are you really okay with me coming along? I could tell you were hesitant, and if you'd rather not have me go, I will decline so you're not in an awkward position."

I'd made him feel unwelcome. *Way to go, Daphne!*

"No, Jasper, don't back out." I laid my hand on his forearm and found the muscles under his nice dress shirt surprisingly tense. As I spoke, the bunched muscle eased under my touch. "I'd love to have you come along," I added for good measure.

"That's the best news I've had all week," he said with genuine pleasure. "After how things went at the mixer, I wasn't sure how you felt, or if you really wanted me to buzz off."

"No, that's not what I want at all," I blurted, announcing the first thing that came to mind for a second time in the same night. To my surprise, he looked unsure of himself, and the tiny crack in his aloof, handsome façade shocked me as much as it excited me. *I affect him, too. It's not just me!* My heart was so eager to jump off the cliff of uncertainty, while my brain wanted to do the smart thing, and not get involved with a man who was passing through.

The dimple that appeared in his cheek at my words, barely shielded by his ever-present five-o'clock shadow, was worth the leap into uncertainty.

"What do you know, then," was all he said, but the undercurrent of the words held much, much more.

Bea hung up the phone, a dreamy expression in her eyes after talking with George. "We should probably all get going, before it gets too late."

"Uh-huh, get going so you can go spend some time with George, you mean?" I gave her a mock-accusing stare. I wasn't mad that she was crazy about my brother, and spending time with him, but it was fun to rib the two of them from time to time. He was still my brother, after all, and some things would never change.

She shook her head. "No, not tonight. I have to open at the shop tomorrow, and I'm going in early since the crowd was so crazy today."

Her disappointed words reminded me of the near-empty restaurant we were sitting in, just the three of us and an upset Janie at the hostess's stand. My resolve to do something about this ridiculous boycott solidified in that moment, seeing the heartbroken look on such a sweet woman's face as she hung her head in her hands.

"Besides, it's late already—it's after nine," she continued, unaware of my wandering thoughts.

"What, really?" I looked down at my phone, surprised to see she was right.

"Time flies when you're having fun, right, Daphne?" Jasper said lightly, and bumped my arm with his elbow in a teasing gesture.

"Apparently it does!" I agreed, shocked with how quickly the night had flown with Jasper at my side.

We all gathered our things, paid Janie, who had put her game face back on, for our delicious dinners. She seemed unaware that anyone had witnessed her moment of self-doubt, but the issue was seared into my brain, and I couldn't let this go without helping make it right. *I guess Celia's not the only meddler in this town.*

The three of us wandered out into the night, and Bea quickly took her leave with a hug for me and a wave for Jasper.

"So, am I safe to assume you'll be visiting Bea bright and early for a morning donut?" Jasper asked mildly as we walked down the sidewalk towards Bert. Jasper hadn't asked first, he'd just fallen into step beside me, as if walking me to my truck was as natural as breathing.

"If I can make it early enough to beat the crowd, definitely."

"Ah, yes. And you've been fighting off a crowd of travelers, too. Well then, I won't keep you. Have a good evening, Daphne." He paused, and for a brief moment, I could see a look of indecision cross his handsome features. Whatever it was he thought, he gave me a nod, before I climbed up into Bert's cab and clicked my seatbelt into place. Once I was settled, he lifted one hand in a good-bye, before turning and slowly crossing the street to where his little black sports car waited.

As I backed Bert out of the space, the first tell-tale cramp hit me like a brick to the uterus. *Ugh, seriously? What timing you have, Aunt Flo.*

SIX

Stirring the Pot

CELIA ANNE MONTGOMERY

I walked out of Jude's with my head a-swirl. Daphne. My word, but that girl had an independent streak a mile wide, and longer than the whole Savannah River. When I overheard those two girls talking about who to take on their trip, the answer was clear as day, and yet there she sat, in complete denial. Well, that just wouldn't *do*. That English boy was plum smitten with her, and she was too love-blind herself to realize it. He barely spoke to a soul in this town, except her.

A long weekend away might be exactly what the doctor ordered, to make those two see what was right in front of them. I might have to do some more encouraging, but sure as you please, I'd help those two see the light. Otherwise, she'd be right where she'd always been, and he'd be off on a new adventure, and they'd both be as miserable as a pig in a desert.

Call it what you want—meddling, nosiness, over-stepping—I couldn't turn off my matchmaker's eye. When I saw a young couple who were perfect for each other, I couldn't sit idly by and watch them make a mess of things. No, sometimes the young folks in this town needed a little *nudge* in the right direction. And who better to provide it? Nobody, that's who.

Now, I had to keep an eye on them until they were sorted out. As I ambled towards my silver SUV to head home for the evening, the possibilities played before me like a Hallmark movie. So many good options, one of them was bound to make them see sense.

SEVEN

Time Flies

Period cramps were Satan's mistress. I swear, when that time of the month rolled around, it felt like somebody somewhere got a kick out of my misery. Or was kicking me in the guts to *cause* my misery. Either way, it was personal. Was I dramatic about it? Of course not. Rolling out of bed half an hour early to get to the agency in time to catch up on my overflowing inbox before the day full of booking appointments began was not my idea of a good time. Doing it with my period in full, raging effect was torment. *Definitely Satan. Sadistic arse.*

I dragged my lagging, pained body to my bathroom and made my way through my morning routine as quickly as I could, which is to say, not quickly at all. Severe endometriosis coupled with PCOS made my life miserable in a lot of ways. Pain, bloating, unpredictable periods, and all the rest were no walk in the park. The worst, though, was knowing I may never have a family of my own.

No, I corrected myself, *I will have a family one day. A family of my own making, if not my own genetics.* It was a promise I'd made myself after the first doctor had told me the severity of my endometriosis meant getting and staying pregnant without medical intervention would be a one-in-a-million chance.

Barc scratching at the bathroom door urged me on and I managed to get myself together enough to let him out and fill his bowl with food. Back to the closet, I grabbed my stretchy-but-don't-look-stretchy work pants, a jewel-green, flowy top and my favorite shiny silver flats. Was it a little excessive given that I spent most of the day behind a desk, where no one saw my feet? Yes. Was that going to stop me from enjoying shoes that glittered like the starry night sky? Not for all the tacos in Mexico. *Mmmm, tacos. Definitely stopping by El Burro's for lunch.* It may have been luxurious to get mid-day takeout, but infinitely worth it to cheer me up.

The thought of fresh tacos piled high with sauteed onions and cheese finally kicked me into gear, and in two minutes flat I was dressed, shod, and letting Barc back in from the back yard.

"Hey, Barc-ie. What a good boy you are. I refilled your bowl—I know you're a growing boy." I scratched him behind the ears, and he thumped the floor with one hind leg appreciatively before trotting over to his bowl and going to town on his breakfast. My stomach rumbled, angry that it had been neglected.

Bert fired up for me on the first try, like always, and I drove towards town rubbing the sleep from my eyes. Before pulling into my usual space behind the travel agency, I drove a bit further down to check the wait at the bakery. My heart sank and my stomach growled at the sight of a line, two people across, all the way down the street to the corner. Even half an hour early, there was no way I'd make it through that before my first appointment arrived.

With a sigh, I weighed my options. Jude's didn't open for two more hours, and Granny's Diner was at the other end of town—plus, if you went in before noon the early birds would never let you out again. Suddenly struck with an idea, I pulled back down to the travel agency, put it in park, and grabbed my phone to text my dearest older brother.

Daph: Hey, bro, help a sister out. Can you bring me two donuts and a coffee?

George-the-Great: Right now?

Daph: Yes, right now. Or, you know, fifty years from now when I die of starvation.

George-the-Great: Sorry sis, I am heading straight to a job site this morning to meet an inspector. Rain check? I'm free tomorrow.

Daph: I was going to let it slide that you changed your name in my phone again, but this clenches it. You're getting a new name.

George-the-Great-anteater: You know you still love me. See you tomorrow, and I'm buying.

Daph: <3

George-the-Great-anteater: *Hugs*

Resigned to my donut-less state, I piled out of the truck with much less enthusiasm than I'd climbed in with. I would just order tacos as soon as the restaurant opened. It was only a few hours. My despairing sigh vanished into the morning air. After unlocking the back door and settling in at my laptop, I pulled up my inbox and quickly started working through the backlog of emails. Luckily most were the standard resort ads, and I could leave those for a less busy time. I found the email from the corporate office with the details of the trip I'd won and read through that quickly. Nervous excitement buzzed in my chest at the idea of four whole days with Jasper. Good, bad, or ugly—it was happening.

I purposefully directed my attention to the next email from Trina with some final decisions for their parents' fortieth-anniversary trip and jotted down notes about what to book for them. About five emails later, I was already over it. I crossed my arms on my desk, and leaned my head down for a moment, trying to give myself a mental pep talk.

Only a few more hours and you can take a break and eat all the tacos you can fit in your stomach. You can make it, Daphne! My stomach grumbled angrily, as if it could hear my thoughts and *soundly* disagreed. Well, too bad, stomach. No tacos until eleven.

I was still bent over, head on my desk, when a knock startled me from my internal argument. I popped up, scarlet hair flying everywhere, to see who was knocking twenty minutes before the agency opened. There at the door with a bakery bag and two coffees in tow, was Jasper. I hurried around the desk, and unlocked the front door to let him in.

"Jasper, hi! . . . What are you doing here?" I asked, taking in his crisp, professional attire. His black button-up shirt formed to his muscular chest in a tantalizing way that barely hinted at the masculine perfection I was quite sure hid beneath it. Dark jeans and a gray blazer made him look like an advertisement for a business casual store that went very, very right. His hair was the only part of him that wasn't all suave perfection, mussed and with a slight curl, it seemed to defy his attempts at styling. Almost as if it was longing to break free from the hair products taming it.

I could help you break free, curls. I would get my fingers in there, and—

"May I come in?" Despite my less-than-exuberant welcome, he gave me a confident grin as he interrupted my train of thought.

"Uh, sure. I mean, yes. Yes, please come in." I stepped aside with a raging flush enveloping my cheeks, and waved him towards my desk, which was messy with loose brochures and my hand-jotted post-it notes regarding various reservations and research items for clients.

"Rough morning?" he asked, and it took me a moment to realize he was referring to finding me face-down on my desk.

"Err, well, yes. But that's not important. Do you need something? Help with planning a trip, or . . . ?" I trailed off, too afraid to ask if maybe he was just here to see me.

"Oh, yes—I need your help with some business arrangements. Can we sit?" he asked, and I sighed internally, but crossed behind my desk and sat, putting on my most professional face.

"Of course, how can I help you, Jasper?"

Rather than answer, he passed me one of the coffees, and then began digging in the bakery bag. Confused for the second time in as many minutes, I stared as he pulled out a blueberry muffin for himself, and then in a smooth motion slid me the bag which, on further inspection, contained not one, but *three* delicious, fresh donuts. And they were my favorite flavors.

"Are these for me?" I asked, questioning the obvious as tears stung my eyes.

"Sure are." He took a sip of his coffee nonchalantly, as if he hadn't rocked my world with his thoughtfulness and near-telepathic timing.

"That's just the nicest thing anyone has ever done for me." To my utter horror, I could hear and feel myself getting choked up. I sniffed, determined not to let any actual tears escape.

"Hey, uhh, are you all right?" For the first time since I'd met him, his cool, calm mien gave way to panic. I looked up to see widened eyes and saw his eyebrows drawn down in concern.

The clear worry snapped me out of my hormonal tears, and instead I burst out giggling. Confusion crossed his handsome face, and I had to cover my mouth with my hand to stop the peals of laughter trying to wrest themselves free of my lips.

"O-kay . . ." he said, as if I'd lost my marbles. Then, proving his endless capacity to subvert my expectations, he started chuckling with me. His deep, masculine laugh permeated the room and washed over me like a physical sensation.

Breathless with laughter, our eyes caught and held. In that joyful moment, it felt like the world stopped spinning. I knew in science class we'd learned about the hypothetical terrible things that would happen if the world came to a screeching halt—but at that instant, I discovered that Mrs. Ahiel was a liar—because the world had stopped dead in its tracks, and the only thing that exploded was the heart in my chest.

"I'm sorry. I'm not crazy, I swear," I insisted, my gaze fixed on his rich brown eyes. They were so soulful, I could stare into them for the rest of my life and not miss a thing.

"I never had any doubt of that," he answered, and my stomach clenched of its own accord.

"I'm just feeling emotional today, and I really love donuts," I stated, probably sounding like a loon.

"Understandable; they're quite tasty." He paused, seeming indecisive. Squaring his shoulders, he asked, "Is everything okay?"

My cheeks burned as I realized that I needed to offer *some* explanation for my zany emotional roller coaster. "Yes—uhm, well—Aunt Flo arrived this morning, and I don't feel amazing. I didn't have time to wait out the ridiculous line at the bakery, and I'd just asked George to bring me donuts, but he couldn't because of work. Oh, hey, we're supposed to be talking about your work travel, huh?" I stopped rambling, taking in his devilishly handsome face, searching for signs of disgust or freak-out at the mention of *womanly issues*. After finding no trace, I stopped talking and waited for him to answer.

"I'm sorry you're not feeling well. If you'd rather I can come back later . . . It's nothing urgent, I only need a round trip flight to the main office in Miami, and then a two-night hotel stay. As talented as you are, I'm sure you could arrange that in your sleep." He smiled, and the sudden appearance of the dimple in his left cheek made my brain lose focus and my breath catch.

"No, no! I'm much better now." I lightly shook the donut in explanation. "I'm happy to arrange it. Which part of Miami?" Switching into business mode was definitely the safest bet with Jasper around, so I clung to the normalcy. Spinning to my computer, I shook my mouse and looked back at him expectantly.

"Ahh, are you familiar with the Brentwood area?" he asked, taking a sip of his coffee.

"Un momento, por favor!" I quickly typed the location into my planning program, and a list of hotel options and the nearest airport popped up.

"You speak Spanish?" He lifted an eyebrow in question.

"Un poquito," I acknowledged while continuing to type. "I'm not fluent, but I think if you're going to see the world, you should make an effort to speak with the locals in their own language. So far I can speak a bit of five languages. It's polite, you know?" I spun the screen so he could see the top choices, and found him studying me with an indecipherable look on his face.

I stared back, trapped in his chocolate gaze. The corner of his lips curled upward a tick. "I agree, it's acknowledging that you've come to their home, and that you're making an effort to know them, instead of wanting to just trample over their lovely destinations and leave."

I couldn't help the smile that tugged at my lips in response. "Yes, exactly. There are so many places that aren't tourist friendly because that's what they expect. But, it doesn't have to be that way. Sure, we all want to see the highlights. The Eiffel Tower, the Great Barrier Reef, the Haeinsa Temple . . . but the culture and the people are every bit as beautiful, and just as worth seeing."

His answering deep chuckle made warmth pool in my belly, and a fluttery shiver traveled down my arms. "I've never met anyone else who's seen that the same way I do. Although, you *are* a seasoned travel agent, so you're more passionate on the topic than most. Wow, that's a nice selection of hotels." He nodded to the screen, and I mentally shook myself.

Focus, Daphne. He's here on business. The fact that he's freaking perfect doesn't mean you can't stay calm and professional.

"Yes! I think you'd really like this one. It's a boutique hotel that was purchased by Hilton, so it has the amenities but still a unique charm that isn't found in a lot of the big chains. But, we can still get you a great deal since it's under their umbrella."

"That's perfect. Can you book me in next month for the twelfth and thirteenth?"

"Sure you don't want to see the rest? Miami has dozens of nice options." I gestured to the list with a flourish.

Jasper shook his head. "Nope, no need. That place looks perfect."

"Consider it done, then. Do you prefer morning flights for business?"

We reviewed the flight options, and a few clicks later, I had him all set for his next trip back to the home office. I hated every second of him leaving afterward—it felt like the beginning of goodbye.

I watched his retreating back in a daze, tracing the outline of his shoulders under the crisp gray shirt he'd worn this morning. *You've got it so, so bad, girl.*

EIGHT

Go, Sports

T he weekend arrived and, with it, the normal invite to my brother's house to watch a baseball
game. Which was code for, "Bring food, and hang
out with Bea while lightly mocking the guys' obsession with dudes in tight uniforms running around
and chasing balls." They didn't see the humor, but
that's what besties were for, and we'd been doing it
since he'd moved into this house a few years ago.
At this point, it was tradition. My standard squash
casserole was riding shotgun in Bert's passenger
seat—standard, because it was the only thing I knew
how to cook.

My eyebrows shot up when I pulled up to George
and Finn's place and spotted an extra vehicle in

the driveway. Heart hammering at the sight of the black two-seater, I looked down and sighed at my green and white raglan tee and cut-off shorts. While they were perfect for the casual brother-hangout occasion, I'd have put in a lot more effort if I'd known Jasper would be here. *Too late now.*

I parked Bert right behind Bea's silver sedan, and mentally coached myself as I walked up the front steps. Pausing, I took two deep breaths before knocking. *So what if he's here? We're friends. He's passing through, and we're both adults. I can be friends with him without reading too much into anything.*

Steeling my spine, I rapped twice on the front door.

George appeared a moment later, smiling as always. "Hey, sis, come on in." He stood to the side and gestured toward the kitchen. "Is that your famous squash casserole?"

I rolled my eyes. "You already know the answer to that, George."

He chuckled at my petulant tone. "One of these days, you might surprise me, and make something else."

"Not likely." I sashayed past him into his little green-clad kitchen and dropped my casserole dish off next to whatever heavenly sugar-dusted concoction Bea had brought. Was it tiramisu? I could never tell. Voices filtered in from the living room, and Finn's cheers assaulted my ears. *Let the fun begin.*

Bea sashayed in, hand on her hip in a joking fashion. "Excuse me, sir, why are you holding up my best friend—shouldn't you be in there watching all those dudes in tight pants with your buddies?"

George snorted. "I'm not holding anybody up. I was just talking with my sister—is that still allowed?" He winked at her and gave me a quick side hug and then did as she asked and walked out of the kitchen and into the living room with the other guys.

Bea lowered her voice in a conspiratorial tone. "So, I take it you saw the extra car out there, right?" her eyebrows drew up in glee.

I bit my lip before answering. "I did . . . Any idea How that happened?"

She shrugged one shoulder noncommittally. "No idea, but I think you should make the best of it, personally."

I groaned and dropped my head into my hands. "That sounds simple, but I feel so awkward. I've never had this problem before, so what is it about *him*"—my voice dropped to a whisper automatically, to avoid anyone overhearing from the other room—"that has me so . . . in knots? Why can't I just relax and be normal?"

Bea tapped her chin idly as she thought it over. "Well, the fact that he gets under your skin means you really care what he thinks. It's how you know he has real potential, and you need to go out on a limb. I mean, if you were capable of being that blasé about him, then what's the point? Didn't you tell me not so long ago that if I never risked anything, I'd never gain anything?" She raised one manicured eyebrow to accentuate her point.

"Yes, yes I did. But that's different. You've known George forever, and he's as steady as a rock, to boot. I have to go and fall for somebody who's a ramblin'-man-free-bird-savant."

"Daph, you know I love you, right?"

"Yes, mom," I responded, voice thick with sarcasm.

"Good, then remember I say this with love. You've fallen for him. You care, and you're interested. You have to take the leap. Open yourself up to the possibility, even if it means getting hurt. Because as long as you keep yourself on the shelf, you're not giving Jasper the chance to show up and be who you're looking for." She thought for a moment before continuing, "Besides, nobody understands the wandering feet better than you. Maybe you two are each exactly what the other needs."

I pursed my lips in agitation as I digested what she'd said. *She's not wrong. It's just so scary.* We stood there in companionable silence for a few moments, and when she realized I was going to keep mulling on it, Bea shifted gears to uncovering dishes of food and setting out paper plates and napkins. I watched her work, efficient as always, until I came to a decision. I could do this. I could be open to the possibilities with Jasper.

With new determination, I rolled my shoulders back, lifted my chin, and stepped out of the kitchen.

I strode into the living room, put at ease by the familiar background noise of a baseball game. Cheers, bats cracking against a ball, and the announcer's voice faded to a drone as I zeroed in on Jasper. He was sitting at the far end of the couch, one foot propped against his knee, and his left arm slung across the back of the couch. His jeans molded enticingly to his long legs, and my eyes traced a line up his torso and across his defined chest. The t-shirt he was wearing looked soft, and the teal really made his brown eyes pop. Jasper looked over from the game with a bored expression, but when he spotted me heading his way the smile that lit his face made my breath hitch.

I stopped a foot away and popped my hip out, resting my hand on it. With my best flirty tone I asked, "Is this seat taken?"

He chuckled. "If it was, I'd give you mine." He patted the couch cushion to his left in invitation.

"Ah, I do love a gentleman. You know, we Southern ladies are trained to spot them at fifty yards."

"Really, now. That sounds like an interesting talent." His eyes twinkled with mischief. "What happens if you spot a rake, then?"

"The kind you garden with, or the kind from historical romance novels?" I parried, not missing a beat.

"Definitely the latter."

"Ahh, very straightforward. Ms. Manners insists that you remove yourself from his presence with all haste, preferably while giving your best haughty look over your shoulder." I twisted away from him and cast my best disparaging glance over my shoulder, and he pretended to wither away from the haughty glare.

"Well, in that case, I'm glad I fall under the 'gentlemen' category." He looked distracted for a moment with his gaze traveling down my face, and then he lifted his hand from the back of the couch, and gently ran a tendril of my hair between his thumb and pointer finger. The silky strand slid free, and I held my breath at the unexpected contact. Our eyes locked again, and the heat rose between us like the Georgia summer moon—hot, bright, and seeming close enough to touch. His fingertips trailed from my shoulder down the outside of my arm, leaving a trail of tingles in their wake. I held my breath as his hand reached mine, and he paused, as if asking permission for something. Acting on instinct, I slowly turned my hand over, and he trailed his fingertips soft as a whisper across my palm, before lacing his fingers with mine. Our eyes never left each other, and in that moment I knew I was a goner.

Warmth tingled its way up my arm, and I willed my brain to think of something intelligent to say, instead of sitting here, staring at his masculine beauty.

"How are you liking Georgia? I know it's a big change from England."

"Yeah, huge change. But, the town has drawn me in. The slower pace, the friendly people. And the sunshine is nice. It's rather rainy back home." One side of his mouth quirked up in a smile and he gave my fingers a gentle squeeze.

"Hmm, well, you won't entirely escape the rain. But, you're right, the people are great. I know a lot of my friends growing up couldn't wait to go somewhere bigger—busier, really—but something about Adele has etched itself on my heart."

"I can see why. Although, Dolly is a real character. Is she always in a faff about things, or is she only angered about the tea? Because, really, you all make tea wrong anyway, so I don't see what she's so bothered about."

I let out a shocked gasp, and raised my unoccupied hand to my chest. I responded with my most dramatic Southern drawl, "Why, I do declare that is *blasphemy*, Jasper Lewis. You take it back this instant."

He snorted and shook his head at my theatrics. "Sorry, Daphne, tea is meant to be served *hot*."

I dropped the act and teased right back. "Well, if that's your biggest complaint, that's not so bad. Maybe you'll stick around a while." I tried to keep the nerves out of my voice, but I felt them burning in the pit of my stomach. *Please say you'll stay; please say you'll stay.*

His expression grew serious, and his eyes softened. "I think I will."

My heart soared at his words, and I couldn't stop the goofy grin that took over my face.

"Good. You should."

Bea's best emcee voice interrupted our light banter from the kitchen doorway—"Let's get ready for FO-O-OD!"

I shook my head at her shenanigans and looked back to Jasper. "Shall we?" I asked, gesturing to the kitchen.

"Let's," he agreed.

"So, Jasper . . ." Bea started as she handed out plates. "What do you think of your first baseball party so far?"

"Oh, it's been top notch. I've never watched it before, but it seems to be more of a family tradition here than a simple sporting event, which I appreciate. Back home we all enjoy rugby, so I can see the appeal." He trailed an unobtrusive fingertip down the back of my arm as he said the words, and goosebumps trailed in its wake.

I resisted the urge to shiver as I dropped a few of the Publix wings on my plate next to the potato salad, and squash casserole.

"So, you're a big family man then, huh?" Finn asked off-handedly as he gnawed on an ear of white corn.

"Yes, my family is quite close, and we never pass up an opportunity to do things together. Especially if it involves a good bashing on the rugby pitch." He grinned at the thought.

"It must be hard on you, being so far away," Bea observed as she handed George the last plate. He planted a kiss on her lips in thanks, and she smiled at him in return, the love clear in their eyes.

"It can be, but we've found ways around it over time. They fly out once a year to wherever I'm working, and I fly there at least once a year, sometimes twice. Then we talk regularly in between. Actually, I'm overdue to show my mum around town. She likes me to do a video call of each new place, and walk her around like a virtual tour guide. I always feel a bit silly, but she loves it so much I can't say no." He shrugged one shoulder and ducked his head, and I was surprised by the show of embarrassment. He'd always seemed so unflappable; I wondered what it was about showing his mom around town that was embarrassing to him? I tucked that thought away to ask him later.

"That's sweet, Jasper." I rubbed his arm in reassurance.

He gave me a crooked smile, and I dropped a few wings onto his plate.

"So, you're a mama's boy?" Finn asks, sarcasm thick in his tone. Without waiting for an answer, he shakes his head and marches back to the TV with his plate.

Jasper doesn't get mad at the observation, just shakes his head at Finn's retreating back.

"Don't mind him, he's leery about mentions of family. I get the impression that his isn't all that close. Frankly, I think it's a defense mechanism." George slaps Jasper reassuringly on the back. "Nothing wrong with loving your mother. Family is important."

"Couldn't agree more, although I'd appreciate it if my mum would back off on the grandkid hunting. Is yours that way, as well?"

I stiffened at the repeat mention of kids but forced myself to relax.

George started laughing, and it didn't seem like he was going to stop any time soon. His face turned red, and a few tears escaped the corners of his eyes before he managed to pull it back together. "Dude, my mom is *obsessed* with getting some grandkids.

She hints almost daily that I should go ahead and marry Bea, so we can start popping out babies."

"Not happening!" Bea interrupts from the end of the counter where she's laying a slice of cake on her plate, right along with the wings and normal food. "I'm not ready for babies anytime soon."

"I know, I know—we're in no hurry." George answers her in a reassuring tone before looking back over at Jasper. "But no, your mom isn't the only one. It's funny, in the teenage years it's all about *not* having babies. You get within spitting distance of thirty, though, and they turn on a dime."

Jasper snorted his agreement. "Yes, that about sums it up. I mean, I want children, of course, but you have to find the right woman first." He gave me a flirty wink. "I can't imagine waiting too terribly long after that, though." Hot dread pooled in my stomach and I had to force a weak smile in response.

There it was—the other shoe. He hadn't even asked me on a date, and he was bringing up kids. The conversation continued to swirl around me, but I stood there like a fallen tree in a riverbed. Water was rushing by, while I lay there stuck and drowning in the memory of a cold doctors office, and the news of my various conditions meaning my reproductive systems weren't quite right. Fifteen-year-old me had known enough to ask what all those long diagnosis names meant for one day having children, and the doctor hadn't looked positive, even then.

He might be joking now, but I'm just going to be a disappointment to him when the baby conversation comes up for real. I might not even be able to have kids, and if I can, it's not going to be this fun, romantic thing. It's going to be doctors and procedures and hormone shots. The frustration and anger I could imagine all over his face with vivid clarity played in my head like a bad movie on repeat. I stood there, dumbstruck, and mentally spiraled. Bea looked up from squeezing dessert onto her plate and noticed my statue routine.

"Do you want a slice?" she offered, and I wordlessly stuck mine out. She slid a piece of gooey chocolate cake right next to my squash casserole, and I couldn't find it in me to be annoyed when they got all up in each other's business on the plate.

"Thanks," I mumbled before turning and leaving the three of them chatting in the kitchen. I sat back down in the single chair next to the couch, facing Finn in his old mauve recliner. He sat with one leg over the arm of the chair, and an arm slung across the back, with his food balanced precariously on the other leg. He didn't notice my mood, and for once I was grateful for his self-absorption.

Several minutes later, Bea, George, and Jasper piled back into the living room to watch the game. Jasper walked back over, and I watched it dawn on him that I hadn't taken the same spot I'd been in before. He turned and started to say something, but I was at my limit. I jumped up and cut him off.

"I think I'm going to head home. I'm not really feeling the baseball tonight. Catch you all later." I dropped my untouched food on the kitchen counter and stared at my feet as I walked out of there as quickly as humanly possible without actually running.

"See you tomorrow!" Bea hollered at my back but thank the good Lord she didn't try to follow me. I wasn't fit for company anymore.

NINE

On a Jet Plane

The time flew by over the next few weeks, and finally it was time to go on our trip. I had ducked and dodged like a soccer goalie, between Bea's hounding, and all of the casual run-ins with Jasper where I'd abruptly made excuses and run like the chicken I was. I'd even seen him every few days, strolling through town, or walking past my agency window. He had stopped and waved, but each time I'd had a customer, so he hadn't come in. The look on his face let me know he wasn't ready to just drop it, though. I had a feeling he was biding his time and giving me some space—after all, we were about to spend four straight days together, so the avoidance had to end. And Bea, well, she had only eased off because I finally convinced her I wasn't ready to talk about it. That conversation was going to come due, and *soon*.

I had mixed emotions about it, given the revelations with Jasper and my own insecurities about how my future path to motherhood would look. How did you even begin to bring that up with someone, when a relationship was barely started? I sure as heck didn't know. It was a textbook case of How to Lose a Guy In Ten Days 101—start talking babies before the second date, and you were S-O-L. Even if the talk was, "Hey, I may not be able to have babies, and if I am it is probably going to be difficult and involve some doctors. Or, you know, adoption might be the best plan."

Ugh. There was just no good way to drop that on someone, and the longer you waited, the worse it got. So, I'd been avoiding him. Not smooth in the least, but the old habits of protecting my heart didn't want to let me go, and I was too chicken to open the door again myself. So, I still had nothing to tell him to explain away my stupid behavior . . . if he still wanted to talk to me after three weeks.

I loaded my bright red weekend suitcase in the truck bed, and then whistled for Barcelona. He came running from where he was sniffing the front bushes, brown ears flapping, and jumped right into Bert's passenger seat with a happy whuffle. I gave him a quick rub behind the ears, accepted his appreciative lick, and shut the door.

After dropping him off at my parents' house so they could spoil him silly for the next four days, I headed over to the bakery. We were all meeting there since Celia had volunteered to drop us at the airport in her delivery SUV. We were going to call a ride, but she'd insisted when she overheard Bea and me discussing it last week.

I wheeled my suitcase through the back door, and the sound of soft country music mingled with happy conversations filtered in from the front of the store. I hesitated for a moment in the neat-as-a-pin back room—Celia was a stickler on the whole "cleanliness is next to Godliness" thing—savoring the moment alone. It was going to be hard to keep my distance from Jasper this coming week, but it was really for the best. He was so intense, so magnetic, and if I wanted any chance of keeping my heart intact, I had to try.

Granted, we'd only held hands. And there was that one moment where I thought he might have been about to kiss me, but I couldn't be sure. The pull between us was so strong that I knew I was on the verge of head over heels. *Sure, Daphne, let's pretend you're still on the verge.* Plus, we were about to spend four uninterrupted days in the same place with no buffer besides Bea and George, and they were no help, as wrapped up as they were in each other.

I rolled my shoulders back and forced myself to shake it off. *You're a grown woman. You control your own relationships, or lack thereof. There is no reason to be hiding in a supply room when there's an amazing vacation waiting for you. You will relax or die trying. Now, it's time to get this show on the road, Daphne!*

Mental pep-talk complete, I strode out of the back room, and did my best to sound more chipper than I felt. "Who's ready to traaaaavel?!" I sang as I jangled my suitcase handle at Bea, George, and Jasper who were all waiting around one of the dainty café tables.

"Oh, I am so ready!" Bea jumped up from the table, and wrapped me in an excited hug.

I returned the hug with one arm, and winked at George over the top of her head. My eyes skittered over to where Jasper was now standing in his signature pose, hands in pockets and rocked lightly back onto his heels. His gaze was warm, but I could also sense a distance between us that hadn't been there before, and I felt the stab of regret straight to my traitorous heart.

I took the cowardly way out, and flitted past him around to Celia, who'd just finished flipping the "Open" sign on the door. She turned and propped one hand on her hip before taking us all in. Her all-too-perceptive gaze landed on me, then flicked over to Jasper, and I could almost swear that I saw a brief flash of disappointment there, but she moved on too quickly to be sure. "Well now, y'all, let's not dawdle. You've got a fancy island to get to." She clapped her hands together once and led us out front to her waiting delivery SUV. George kissed me on the cheek as he took my suitcase and loaded it into the back with the other three already waiting there. Bea took shotgun, and I climbed into the back where I was sandwiched in between Jasper and George. The heat of Jasper's thigh pressed against mine put me on high alert, but I pretended not to notice as Celia pulled out of the parking lot of the Sweet Nothings Bake Shop.

Here we go.

The trip to the airport was quick and uneventful. Our moods were bright as the guys unloaded the suitcases curbside, while us girls supervised. As they wheeled them off to the waiting airline employees, Celia loosely hooked my arm through hers and guided me a few steps away from Bea.

"Daphne, you and I need to have a little chat," she said in a hushed, no-nonsense tone.

"Uhm, is everything okay?" I asked, surprised by the usually jovial woman's change of mood.

"No, it frankly is not. What is going on between you and that handsome British boy?" Her stare pinned me in place, and I resisted the urge to squirm.

"What do you mean?" I hedged, not sure what to say.

She sighed. "Daphne, dear, you don't have to tell me if you don't want to. But I know the look I saw on his face earlier today, and it told me you've stomped on his heart somehow. You've both been moping for weeks, and it's downright painful to watch you dance around each other. I don't know the details, and I don't need to. But I'll tell you this, there is a man out there—and it may not be Jasper, only you can decide that—who you simply won't be able to let go of. If you decide wrong, and let Jasper go only to later realize it was him—that he was the *one*—you'll spend every cotton-pickin' day of forever kicking yourself for it." She paused, and my heart clenched as the truth of her words sank in. "And Daphne, don't be one of those people thinking there's always another chance. Some doors, once closed, are closed for good—I don't get the sense that he's a man looking to mess around." She gave me one firm nod, and then climbed into the car, honked to get the rest of the group's attention, and drove off with a graceful wave.

My practiced cheerfulness had left me, and all I felt inside was twisted up in knots. Celia had missed one key thing despite her keen observations. I didn't want to let him go, but I was pretty sure that eventually, he'd be the one to leave me. And that was the worst pain I could imagine. No, it was better to head it off before it ever got there. *Wasn't it?*

As we went through the check-in process at the airport, we settled into the familiar patterns of traveling. Drop luggage, chat through TSA checks, and explore the little shops around the Savannah airport. While I kept a friendly distance between Jasper and me, I was constantly aware of him. It was like I had my own personal radar that was tuned to his presence. One little clothing shop had a nice rack of sunglasses I was flipping through and checking out in the tall, skinny mirror. I tipped them down, and spotted Jasper and George across the shop, looking at tourist t-shirts. George held one up that said, "Came, Saw, Ate Peaches" and they both laughed. Two peas in a man-pod.

I was so engrossed in watching them from behind the sunglass stand that I didn't hear Bea approach from the side.

"Girl, you have got it so bad." I jumped sky high and knocked a pair of bright green glasses off the stand which went clattering to the floor. "Are you ever going to tell me what happened between you two? It seemed like you were finally starting to warm up to him, and then, slam! Door closed." She narrowed her eyes at me, as if she could read the truth from my brain herself if she concentrated hard enough. I picked up the green glasses and tucked them back into their holes on the display.

"Nothing happened, Bea, and that's the truth. Let's just have a nice time on this trip, and not worry about it. Okay?" I gave her my most reassuring smile, but she didn't buy it.

"Uh-huh. A nice time. You won't be able to avoid him the whole trip. Grand Cayman isn't *that* big of an island."

I snorted. "I'm not avoiding anyone, Bea."

My bestie didn't dignify that with a response. Instead she grabbed a pair of black, sparkly shades and wandered over to the cashier.

I watched her walk away, and then my eyes swiveled back to George and Jasper of their own accord. They weren't where I'd left them. George was perusing the snack stand, and Jasper was heading straight towards me, a determined look on his face.

Oh crap. Oh crap, oh crap, oh crap!

"Daphne, how are you this morning? It feels like it's been ages since we've caught a moment to talk." His tone was pleasant, but there was an undercurrent to it that I couldn't quite pin down.

Feeling a bit like a trapped animal, I struggled to match his calm veneer. "Oh, I'm fine . . . You know, things have been crazy lately at work." Awkward silence ruled for a minute as he studied my expression, but I rushed to fill it. "Good time for a vacation." I bit my bottom lip, the nerves needing an outlet.

"I see," he said softly. "Well then, you're in the right place." He tapped the top of the sunglass display twice, then turned on his heel and walked off. I watched him go, a pit the size of the cinnamon roll forming in my gut as I realized the emotional undercurrent I'd been unable to place before. Disappointment. Somehow, that was worse than the anger or annoyance I'd expected. It never occurred to me that by pulling back and protecting myself, I'd disappointed him—*hurt* him—and that discovery didn't sit well with me.

Bea strolled back over with a small plastic bag holding her new glasses, and a paperback for the flight. "Did you make a decision?" She gestured to the array of sparkly glasses, which I'd completely forgotten.

"Yes," I answered with new resolve, "I did."

I attempted to find Jasper alone for even a moment before time to board so that I could explain, but he studiously made himself unavailable, once even ducking into the men's room in what I was *sure* was a flat-out avoidance technique. I gritted my teeth at the sting of that memory as the fresh-faced flight attendant scanned our e-boarding passes. *It's your own fault; you've avoided him for weeks—what did you expect?*

"Business or pleasure?" Drew—according to his nametag—tried to make a conversation, and I smiled weakly in return.

"Pleasure—just a quick getaway."

"That's the best kind, with the right company." His grin showed off straight, white teeth, but despite his tan and overall good looks, I wasn't looking at him *that way*.

"Definitely." I didn't expound, as I didn't want to encourage the conversation, but Drew didn't seem to notice my disinterest.

"I'll actually be staying in Cayman for a few days, myself. Maybe we could look each other up while we're there?"

For a moment, I just blinked at him in surprise, unsure of what to say. This never happened to me. "Uhm, sorry, I'm traveling with friends." I gestured to my group, all holding their boarding passes as well.

"That's no problem, the more the merrier." He winked at me, and I heard Bea chortle behind me as I moved up the jetway towards the plane. I stopped right before the first bend to wait for them, but out of Drew's earshot. The three of them walked up, and there was a very smug look on Bea's face. I raised one eyebrow in question, but she gave a tiny shake of her head. She abandoned George to link her arm with mine and whispered, "Later."

We boarded the flight without incident and settled in with the guys on one side of the aisle and the girls on the other. After the pre-flight instructions and as we were taxiing down the runway, Bea made a quick glance across the plane to ensure the guys were occupied, before leaning in to whisper in a conspiratorial tone.

"So . . . you're not the only one who's got it bad today," she teased.

I couldn't help my eye roll. "Uh-huh. That Drew guy was not taking the hint. That literally never happens to me. The one time I've got an audience, somebody decides to chat me up."

She snorted. "Uh, not what I meant. You walked off, Drew politely scanned our passes, and Jasper—in that delectable accent, no less—says, 'She's taken, mate, don't bother.'" She pantomimed dropping a microphone.

My jaw dropped. "Are you serious?"

"Dead serious!"

This time it was me sneaking a glance across the aisle, wondering what Jasper was thinking, after the confusing morning we'd had. *Maybe I haven't completely blown it?*

As if he felt me spying on him, his gaze flicked up to mine and I froze, trapped in his gorgeous brown eyes. Bea's sharp elbow snapped me back into reality, and I quickly looked away. Snatching up the in-flight magazine, I pretended to be engrossed until the attendants came to ask about drinks. I flipped all of the pages, but I couldn't remember a word I'd read by the time I ordered my Coke from a—thankfully—different flight attendant.

Bea contentedly ate her pretzels and flipped through her paperback at a rapid clip, while I stared out the window and listened to my travel playlist while sipping my drink as our flight drew to a close. Kokomo might have been considered an oldie at this point, but it was still one of my all-time favorite travel songs, and I had listened to it at least twice by the time we touched down in Grand Cayman. That familiar bump-bump of the wheels on pavement caused a flurry of excitement to erupt in my belly. Just like a kid in the back of a car on a long road trip, my excitement at being here wouldn't be denied. Did my brain then immediately skitter to the thought of *now I'm going to interact with Jasper again!*? Yes. Would I admit it to a single soul? Heck naw.

We waited semi-patiently as the rows ahead of us emptied, and then it was our turn. Grabbing my carry-on, I shuffled out into the aisle behind George and Bea. Jasper, ever the gentleman, insisted that I go ahead of him. We hurried off the plane, and out into the thimble-sized airport. George stalled once we'd fished our luggage off the single carousel.

"Where to now, Daph?"

"Follow me, we're heading to the resort's booth." Taking charge, I led the way to the little curtained alcove for Swaying Palms Resort. A local woman in a resort uniform ushered us in, seated us in plush yellow striped chairs, and offered us all iced drinks. After showing our IDs, she pre-checked us into the resort, and called the van driver to come and get our luggage for us. She walked to the doorway to wait for him, leaving us to ourselves for a moment.

"So, this is swanky," Bea commented, indicating the frilly drinks and the huge photographic wall of white sand beaches and turquoise water with the resort's signature yellow-striped cabanas.

"Very," George agreed.

"We're definitely getting the VIP treatment. Is that because you're a travel agent, Daphne?" Jasper asked.

"Oh, no. This is the kind of service we expect when we send clients out, every time. If we get reports of bad service, we don't send repeat business, so the resorts we recommend work very hard to keep the best reputation."

"Makes sense, but I'm still impressed." George winked at me.

I rolled my eyes, but deep down I was flattered. It's always nice when people appreciate your work. "Well, hold onto your panties, because we're only getting started—I'm your cruise director for four whole days."

"That shouldn't sound ominous, should it? Why do I imagine evil villains laughing in my mind after you say that?" Bea asked, sounding mock concerned.

"Muahahahaha—we're going to practice the samba on repeat for four whole days," I threatened while tapping my fingers together and giving them my best villainous stare. They had the nerve to look unafraid.

Jasper chuckled, but was saved from having to comment by the return of the resort representative.

"Okay, Andersons! Your driver has loaded the luggage and is ready for you. Welcome to Grand Cayman, and have a wonderful stay!" She waved us off with a huge smile and refills for the road.

Ten

The Plunge

Paradise had a name, and it was "Swaying Palms Resort." As soon as we got out of the van, the smell of the crisp salt air hit us. The sand was white, the water was the most gorgeous shade of turquoise fading into blue you've ever seen, and the people were so, so friendly. After picking up our room keys, it was a short walk up to our adjoined suites. Jasper said he wanted to unpack and unwind from the trip. Bea and George wanted to go exploring around the property, and as soon as they were off I stretched out in a lounge chair in the shade of our private balcony with my e-reader. Breeze blowing my hair gently under my floppy hat. Not a care in the world. It was utter perfection. Well, almost.

After an hour or so of leisurely reading, I heard the sliding glass door open behind me. Without looking I hollered to Bea, "Get out here girl, and tell me about your exploring! But, you know, skip the parts about making out with my brother—I don't need to know about that," I added with a wave.

A masculine chuckle shocked me into turning around. There he was, breathtaking in a blue-and-white-striped button-up and casual linen shorts. Jasper padded over on bare feet, and settled into the lounge chair next to mine, but sideways so he was facing me instead of sprawled out. The butterflies in my stomach took flight the instant our eyes locked, but I did my best to ignore them. *Calm it down or I will digest you, butterflies.*

He settled his elbows on his knees and fixed me in an intense gaze. "I think we should talk." He paused, took in my cut-off jean shorts and tank top, as well as the forgotten e-reader in my hands. "Unless, of course, you'd prefer I come back later . . . ?"

Ever the gentleman, he offered me a way out. "No, now is fine. Uhm, what do you want to talk about?" I set the book on the patio next to me, and rolled onto my side so I was facing him.

He sighed, and looked out at the water for a moment. "Where to even begin?"

I reached over with my leg and poked him gently with an outstretched toe. "We're on vacation—you're not supposed to look so serious, you know."

He turned back to me and smiled lazily at my teasing. "I can't help it, there's this girl who's got me tied up in knots, and I can't seem to figure out what to do or say around her from one minute to the next." He ran a hand across his chin, rubbing the light dusting of stubble showing there in frustration.

"I see," I hedged, unsure how to respond.

"What's going on, Daphne? Have I done something to upset you, or offend you? We had just made a connection, and it seemed like we were both into it and feeling the mutual attraction, and then in a blink you shut me out. I have been over it in my head at least a hundred times. I've tried to approach you at least a dozen times in the weeks since, but you won't give me anything." His chocolate eyes searched mine, and the look there was so sincere that it made my heart stutter.

"I—" I started, but immediately snapped my mouth closed again. Could I really tell him? Lay it all out there, and then spend the next four days avoiding him if he wanted nothing else to do with me?

Or spend the next four days in paradise, enjoying it together, if he still wants to get to know you. The tiny, hopeful voice in my head scared me.

He reached over and brushed my bottom lip with his thumb, the casual touch sending goosebumps scurrying down my arms and a delicious shiver down my spine. "Talk to me, or you're going to bite your beautiful lip clear off."

Steeling my nerves, I sat up so I could talk with him eye to eye. "No, you didn't do anything wrong, Jasper. I got spooked, and acted like a chicken." I barely resisted the urge to drum my fingers on the lounger anxiously.

"Spooked?" He seemed confused. "If it was something I did or said, you can tell me. I won't be angry, I promise."

"I don't know if I'll be able to have kids. Ever. I have a condition—well, actually two conditions—that will make it difficult. Not impossible, necessarily, but it could be. I don't know."

His eyebrows shot up, and dread climbed up the back of my throat at the reaction.

He was silent for a beat before he said, "Okay, go on."

Forcing my tone to stay even, I continued, "We were at the baseball party, having a great time, and then you made the comment about kids, and how when you found the right person, you wouldn't want to wait to start a family. Hearing how important family is to you, and knowing about my health issues, I just . . . panicked. I didn't want to keep growing something between us and get attached, only to see your disappointment when I eventually told you and you inevitably broke it off." I stared at my toes, unable to meet his eyes as the last words slipped out.

He was silent for an excruciatingly long moment. Then I felt a fingertip under my chin, and he guided me up so that my eyes were once again level with his.

"Daphne, I'm sorry to hear about your health conditions." He paused, and I internally braced myself for what I knew was coming. He was a nice guy, he'd at least be kind about breaking it off. "However, that in no way lessens my interest in you, or my desire to get to know you better."

Shock filtered through me at his words, and I blinked twice, unable to respond.

"Was that the only thing that was bothering you?" He searched my eyes, as if trying to suss out any further secrets.

Swallowing hard, I debated whether or not to mention the fact that, at best, any relationship with him would be temporary. Bea's words about taking risks and making leaps ran through my head, and in that moment, I decided to swing for the fences. He *was* worth it to me, even if it was only for a while. I couldn't bring myself to think I'd be worse off for getting to know him, maybe even loving him. I met his gaze and the rich brown was so deep, I thought I might get lost. Mustering all my courage, I answered, "Yes, that's all."

"Well, then, I hope you'll be open to the idea of spending some more time with me on this trip? I'd like the chance to get to know you better." His mouth lifted in a half smile, and when he raised the ends of a lock of my hair and twirled it between his fingers I wanted to curl up in his lap like a puppy. I resisted, *barely*.

"I'd like that," I finally squeaked out once my brain synapses started firing again.

This time, his smile was blinding. "Excellent. Well, now that that's settled, why don't you get back to that book, and I'll do the same?" He lifted a post-apocalyptic novel, which I hadn't noticed, from his side, and swung around to settle back into the lounge chair.

I nodded, grabbed up my e-reader and unlocked it. With my head in the clouds, it was awfully hard to pay any attention to what the heroine of my book was up to . . . but I think she'd have forgiven me if she saw the fine specimen of a man sitting next to me.

That night we had a dinner reservation at the on-site restaurant. As Bea and I left our room to head down, my little black dress skimmed my knees, and the lace-edged vee neckline added the perfect blend of femininity and mystery. Black, jeweled sandals completed my resort casual dinner look. But on the inside, I was nothing near casual. Getting dressed for a nice dinner out was always fun, but tonight it felt like I was dressing for Jasper. Would he like my dress? Would he appreciate the effort I'd put in to look nice for him? I blew out a nervous breath.

"So, how do you want to play the seating arrangements tonight? Couples? Girls versus guys? Let the chips fall where they may?" I'd caught Bea up on the situation when we were in the bathroom curling our hair, and she'd squealed so loudly that I'm pretty sure the guys heard us through the wall. I wasn't going to confirm that, though, because, *awkward*.

"I think I'm going to let him take the lead. If he sits next to George, no problem. If he sits next to me, excellent."

"He's going to sit next to you, because he's not an idiot," she announced as our sandals slapped down the stairs.

"I guess we'll find out. Are you liking the trip so far?" I asked, changing the subject to more solid ground.

"Loving it! Can't wait to get out tomorrow and sprawl on the beach like a lizard."

"Why a lizard?" I wrinkle my eyebrows in confusion. Lizards aren't usually associated with the beach, unless you count iguanas.

"You know that feeling you get where you're outside soaking up the sun, and it feels divine? Like you're just absorbing the heat and you can feel it all over like a magical blanket of vitamin-D-infused goodness?"

"Bea, I'm a redhead. The sun doesn't love *me* like that."

"True. Anyways, I always thought that must be what lizards feel like when they're out there lying on a rock."

"You are weird, but I still love you," I responded as we arrived at the restaurant.

She shook her head at me, but didn't argue. She crossed the parquet foyer to George's side, and took his outstretched hand. I locked eyes with Jasper, and his genuine smile warmed me from my toes to the tips of my hair. *Who needs to be a lizard in the sun—I'll bask in the glow of Jasper, instead.*

I slowly crossed over to him, and he reached out a hand and ran it from my elbow to my wrist; the soft touch, a whisper of promise.

"You look absolutely ravishing this evening, Daphne."

Suddenly shy, I ducked my head. "Thank you, you look pretty fantastic, yourself," I said, running my eyes up his khaki shorts and crisp white button-up. "Island life seems to agree with you so far."

"Oh, I could definitely get used to this," he agreed, and linked his fingers with mine, giving them a little squeeze.

"Right this way, please," a yellow-uniformed hostess called, and led us into the dining room. The tables were well spaced, and giant painted pots filled with deep green palm fronds around the perimeter of the room gave it a tropical vibe. The open dance area already had a few couples swaying to the live music. When she stopped at our table, Jasper pulled out a low-backed rattan seat for me. I settled into it, and he selected the one directly next to me, across from George.

Bea had a smug, I-told-you-so gleam in her eye as she picked up her menu. We all perused the options in companionable silence for a few minutes before George asked, "What's soursop juice?"

"Mmm . . . I know it's a native fruit, but I haven't tried it before."

"What, are you telling me that our travel agent extraordinaire actually doesn't know something about the local cuisine?" Jasper asked with mock outrage.

I shook my head. "Nope, I know it's green and prickly looking and that was as far as I ever looked into it."

"Well, clearly we must try it," Bea interjected.

"Must we, though?"

"Yes," she insisted.

A waiter in a striped apron arrived at our table in time to ask in a lilting accent, "Ahh, I love a spirited group! What must we try this evening?"

"Soursop juice?" George said.

The man laughed. "Are you sure about that, my man? You sound scared."

We all laughed at his accurate observation, and ordered four soursops.

"So, Jasper, obviously you are a world traveler for work. Where all have you been?" Bea asked.

"Oh, loads of places. In the US alone I've worked in California, Texas, and now Georgia. In England pretty much all over, and once or twice to Germany and eastern Europe. The building standards vary from country to country, so it's always a new challenge."

"It sounds like it," I agreed.

"That's an impressive list. I've only been out of Georgia a few times, always at Daph's insistence." George commented.

"Anywhere on your list that you've wanted to go, but haven't yet?" I asked.

Jasper looked thoughtful for a moment before answering, "Yes, New Zealand. Opportunities are rare there, but it's my dream job. The island is beautiful, and the people are unique. That one probably won't ever happen, though. My company only has one client there, and those jobs only go to the engineers with the highest seniority."

I felt guilty for the relief that flooded me at hearing he wouldn't likely be called *that* far away. Texas was at least in the same hemisphere. "Well, you can always go for fun, if not work. Australia is next on my list, and New Zealand is really close. Most people visit both."

"True, I haven't done much traveling for fun in the last five years. When you're always on the move, staying in one place tends to be more of a draw." He shrugged before adding, "I have to say, I'm already reconsidering my position on that and we've only just arrived."

The waiter dropped off four, frosty glasses with a pale, milky drink in them, and lime wedges on the side. We all ordered our meals, and then stared at the glasses as he left.

"Who's going first?" I asked, staring skeptically at my glass.

"Nope, we're all doing it together, no wimping out." Bea raised her glass. "To the Caymans!"

"To the Caymans," we all responded in chorus, and took tentative swigs.

"Oh my word," I was the first to say. "This is . . . *amazing*." I took another long drink, and the fruity, milky concoction lit up all my taste buds.

"It really is!" Bea gushed.

The guys nodded their agreement.

"And you chickens weren't going to try it," Bea tsked.

"Hey, I've been to enough places to know that not every delicacy is delicious, okay? Healthy skepticism is a survival tactic."

"Yeah, but think about what you'd have been missing out on if you weren't willing to try something new." The look she gave me was about more than a glass of delicious juice. I peeked at Jasper out of the corner of my eye, and knew she was spot on. I'd been holding myself back—in more ways than I ever realized—out of fear.

The rest of the meal passed in great conversation, and by the end I felt happier than I'd been in months. Beautiful surroundings, good food, and better company could do that to a girl, it seemed.

The musicians had really upped their game as the night went on, and I was swaying in my seat to the beat when Jasper leaned over and whispered in my ear.

"Dance with me?" I felt the brush of his breath on my cheek, and shivered in response.

I nodded, and he held out a hand for mine, and led me onto the floor. He placed his hands gently on my hips, and I put mine lightly behind his neck. We slowly rotated to the island rhythm, and for a while, the world narrowed into just us, there on the dance floor. We fit together perfectly, his head a bit above mine, and in that moment of melting into his solid chest, all my worries drained away one by one. His warmth radiated through the thin satin of my dress like the sun on a damp day, and the gentle heat may as well have been a cattle brand straight into my heart. He was seared into my very being, without even trying.

Bea and George begged off after half an hour, but Jasper and I stayed and danced until the band called it quits for the night. When we finally left the restaurant, pale moonlight brushed each of the endless white steps back up to our room. We walked slowly, hand in hand, in no hurry to get to sleep despite the very late hour.

Jasper stopped climbing the steps, and tugged me over to the railing to look out over the water. "Have you ever seen a sight like that?"

The moon hung full in the sky, reflected off the inky waves in a near-perfect twin image. "No, never." I answered.

"It's the second-most breathtaking thing I've seen tonight." His voice came out hushed, and I turned in question.

"Second?"

He tucked a strand of hair behind my ear, and the warmth in his eyes left no doubts to his meaning. "Second." We laced our fingers back together and finished the climb to our rooms. We stopped in front of my door, and I suddenly felt shy.

"I had a great time tonight," I murmured.

"I did too. Probably my best night yet."

"*Probably*?" I teased.

He leaned down and closed the few inches between us, placing his hands on the door on either side of my head. "Just about perfect, actually." His lips pressed against my temple, and I couldn't help the shiver that snaked through me in response.

"There's only one thing I can think of that would make it better," he continued, pressing a kiss on the other temple, and I had to remind myself to breathe.

"What's that?" I squeaked out.

His eyes traced a path down to my lips. "May I kiss you, Daphne?"

"Technically you already did . . ." I pointed out, and then mentally kicked myself for bringing my sarcasm out to play at this moment, of all moments. Thankfully though, he laughed.

"True, but not what I meant." His eyes danced with humor.

"In that case, yes," I answered, biting my lip in anticipation.

Ever so slowly, he leaned down. One of Jasper's hands left the door, and came up to tenderly cup my jaw. My eyes fluttered closed at the touch, and then his lips were on mine. Softly at first, he grew bolder after a moment and my pulse pounded in my veins in exhilaration. His lips were firm yet soft, and I never wanted him to stop kissing me. When he broke away, he rested his forehead against mine, and I wrapped my arms around him in a hug. He slid his arms down and hugged me back, the steady beat of his heart became my new favorite sound.

When we eventually parted, he smiled and said, "Now it's my best night ever."

It felt like I melted into a puddle, but somehow my boneless legs got me inside our room. I slipped the door shut behind me, and sunk back against it. As I stood in the dark, enveloped in the lingering scent of his cologne, I knew that my heart would never be the same again.

ELEVEN

The Sand & The Sea

B eing a travel agent didn't actually mean I was as adventurous as everyone seemed to assume. I mean, being in a new place and trying new things *was* an adventure—which was why, when the guys chose parasailing as their morning activity, I was very confident in my decision not to risk life and limb along with them. Bea and I chose instead to lie on the beach where we could relax, get some sun and book time, and still see their shenanigans on the water. Win, win, win. Then, in the afternoon, we'd head out as a foursome in a glass-bottomed boat and check out all the beautiful sea life.

There was just one teeny-tiny fly in the proverbial soup. I stared in the mirror at the red, polka-dotted bikini, and adjusted the strap for the eighty-seventh time in the last twelve minutes. It looked fine, same as it had the first time. With a sigh, I gave up my adjusting and exited the bathroom to grab my cover up. I slid it over my head and headed out to the patio where Bea was waiting, paperback in hand.

"Ready, chica?" I asked.

"Yep, I have been for ten minutes. What took you so long?"

"Just getting ready. Perfection takes time, you know." I waved vaguely at my hair, which was artfully twisted up on the back of my head.

"Well, you look great as always. Let's hit the sand!" She stood and stretched lazily.

Bags in tow, we traversed the now-familiar steps to ground level, and then wandered along a twisty, palm-shaded path to the beach. My toes sunk into the warm sand, and I sighed in bliss. I didn't know what it was about sand between your toes and ocean waves dancing in the background that was so perfectly relaxing, but it was. We slipped and slid through the fine white sand down to the front row of yellow-striped lounge chairs set under matching umbrellas. Finding a set that suited us—mine shaded, Bea's sunny—we dropped our beach bags, and got comfortable.

I quickly spritzed myself with sunscreen, while Bea shook her head. "Your chair is in the shade. Why do you need sunscreen already?"

"Do you see my hair? It means my skin hates the sun. If all those vampire books were real, I would *be* a vampire with this coloring. Besides, I don't tan, I just freckle."

"Well, suit yourself. I'll put some on in a little while." She stretched out on the chair and scanned the water for our guys.

Our guys. Even the thought sent a little thrill through me, and I quickly tossed the spray aside and joined her in inspecting the waves for signs of a certain parasailing hottie. Finding nothing yet, I turned to Bea. "They're probably still watching a safety video."

"Probably. That's okay, more girl time for us." She lowered her glasses on her nose so she could peer over them at me. "So . . . you came in pretty late last night. How long did you two dance?"

I felt the blush heating my cheeks at the memory of slow dancing all night, followed by the most spectacular kiss of my life. "Pretty late, we didn't leave until the music stopped."

"Ooh la la, that's a good night. Although your feet probably aren't too happy." She slid her glasses back up and resumed watching the waves.

"Not really, but it's been way too long since I had a night of dancing." My lips curled up in a smile involuntarily, and she instantly latched on.

"That looks like more than just a good night of dancing, and you better spill."

"For starters, it was a *great* night of dancing, followed by him walking me back to our rooms . . . and ending with the single best kiss of my entire existence."

"Shut. Up!" She jumped upright, and knocked over her water bottle. "Tell me everything."

I couldn't help but laugh at her enthusiasm, but I gave her the full play-by-play, punctuated by her squeals of excitement. When I was done, she gushed.

"I knew it! I knew it, I knew it! Didn't I know it?"

"You did, curse you," I admitted begrudgingly.

"Uh-uh, you can't curse the one who steered you right—right into Jasper's strong, British arms." She batted her eyelashes in mock flirtation.

"Fine, I don't curse you. Just, play it cool, okay? It's so new. I'm trying to just take it slow and let things unfold on their own, you know?" Nerves of something going wrong assaulted me, but I shook them off. Everything was fine—better than fine!

"Of course, I'm just giving you a hard time. It's great to see you open yourself up, take some chances after so long of keeping guys at arm's length. Speaking of opening up, that bathing suit looks amazing on you."

I snorted. "Yours looks good too. Maybe too good, George might swallow his tongue when he sees you later."

She cackled with glee. "Good, he's always so calm and perfect, it will be nice to see him rattled for once. Why were we so embarrassed of these, anyways? They are pretty, and flattering."

I fingered one of the ruffles that ran along the bikini bottom as I thought about it. "It wasn't about whether or not we rocked the suits, it was the age. Think about it—what *wasn't* awkward as a teenager? I mean, yeah, we wanted to attract some attention, but we were still growing into these fine figures of ours. I was nowhere near confident, and this suit just made me feel like a walking billboard displaying all my insecurities for other people to judge. Now . . . it's just a bathing suit."

She was silent so long I thought she'd fallen asleep, so her answer surprised me. "You're pretty wise sometimes, you know that?"

"Don't you forget it," I sassed, and then closed my eyes to bask in the glorious warmth as the sound of crashing waves erased all of my stress.

I can't say what woke me, but my brain was mush, and there was a hot, scratchy blanket on me. I moved my leg, but the blanket wouldn't come off. No, *that's not right.* I reached up and rubbed my eye only to run into sunglasses. My eyes flipped open like a switch, and three things hit me at once—one, I was outdoors; two, the sun was blasting me in the face; three, my skin was on fire. I sat up with a lurch, and looked over to see Bea sprawled out and snoring in her chair, too.

With a groan, I dug through my beach bag for my phone, only to see we'd been asleep for several hours. My shade patch had moved, and now encompassed half of Bea, but *none* of me. My skin felt tight, hot, and angry, but at least it didn't look so red yet. Maybe my sunscreen held out?

"Bea, wake up! I need to go back in."

"Okay, we will in a minute," she mumbled.

Ugh, the girl could sleep through a marching band. Before I could begin the next phase of waking up sleeping Bea, I heard my brother call out.

"Hey, Daph! Did you see us? Wasn't that awesome?!" I spotted him and Jasper walking across the sand, grins stretched wide.

"Uhm, well . . ." I started, but he cut me off in his excitement.

"The safety stuff took *forever*, but man was it worth it! There is nothing like that wind in your face, and the view! You can really see some amazing stuff up there."

"It was superb," Jasper agreed. "You would have loved it."

They finally arrived at our chairs, and George took in the still-fast-asleep Bea, and let out a low whistle as he walked over to her.

A fourth thing connected in my brain, and I remembered the tiny bikinis we were both wearing. Cheeks turning red for a whole 'nother reason, I met Jasper's gaze.

He gave me a lopsided smile, and dropped into the sunny lounger next to me. "So, shall I take it from your confused expression and Bea's state of sleep that you two may have missed our grand parasailing adventure?" The question was punctuated with a single-eyebrow lift.

"Unfortunately, yes. I am glad to hear you had fun, though!" I tried to keep my tone light, and ignore the angry burn crawling across my skin like fire.

"We did. It was a once-in-a-lifetime experience."

"Well, I'm sorry we missed it."

"It's okay. They videoed it for us, so you can still see it if you want."

"Oh, yeah, that would be great. Maybe when we get back we can have a watch party or something." A hint of discomfort must have leaked into my voice, because his eyes sharpened and he looked me up and down.

"Is everything all right?"

"Yes, everything's okay, but I need to go up. I'm all sunned out." I tried to give him a reassuring smile, but it may have been a grimace.

"Come on then, I'll help." He jumped to his feet, and gathered up my bag and abandoned e-reader before I could even peel myself from the chair.

"Bea's still out. I was trying to wake her, but—"

"She's pretty much impossible to get up. Don't worry, I've got her." George cut me off. I looked over, and rather than wake her he had stolen a second umbrella that wasn't in use and placed it so she was fully shaded, and then claimed the lounge chair on her other side, as well as her sandy, abandoned paperback.

"Thanks, George." I stood slowly, trying not to jostle anything, and fished my cover up from the beach bag slung over Jasper's shoulder.

I gritted my teeth before lifting it over my head, but still couldn't help the sharp hiss as it settled over my shoulders. I was definitely burnt. *Ugh.*

We slowly walked back up the beach, and a blissful sigh escaped me when we reached the shady, blissfully cool path back towards the rooms.

"So, it seems like you may have gotten a bit too much sun," Jasper observed with a delicate tone.

"Just a bit," I agreed. "Unfortunately we slept long enough that my shade patch moved.

"Ahh, that would do it."

"It's okay, though. It doesn't look that bad. A cool shower and some aloe, and I'll be good to go." I'm not sure if I was lying to him, or myself. Probably both.

"Good, I'd hate for you to be miserable the rest of the trip. I've had a few second degree sunburns myself, and it's about as awful as you can feel."

We walked in companionable silence for a few minutes and while my pace must have been painstakingly slow for him, he didn't complain.

Eventually, he spoke again. "So, is this *the* bikini I heard so much about?"

I groaned. "I think you already know the answer to that."

His chuckle made my belly flip-flop. "Well, it looks great on you, and I must admit I'm a bit jealous thinking of all those teenage boys who must have drooled over you in your teen years. You would have certainly knocked my socks off as a teen." He sounded a bit sheepish at the confession, and it only made me fall for him harder.

"Teen Daphne would have been very pleased to hear that teen Jasper approved. I'm sure you were just as handsome back then." I appreciated the light conversation. He could have made me feel awkward, but instead he'd evened the playing field, and I loved his thoughtfulness.

A surprised bark of laughter escaped him, and he shook his head. "No, I'm afraid I was a rather gangly teen. Also, this hair is a bit wild, so more often than not I had a right cloud of frizz on a too-long face."

I eyed him skeptically but couldn't see it. "You'll have to provide photo proof of that, mister. I don't believe for a second you were ever anything less than perfect."

He chuckled. "My mum would just love that, which is exactly why we won't be telling her of your request."

"That sounds like a challenge, to me."

"No, not a challenge. I see that gleam in your eye, and I am not having it," he teased, and I laughed.

"I bet Celia could get me that photo. She can get anything out of anyone—it's her super power."

He shivered. "That woman is dangerous, for sure. She always seems so sweet and delicate, but somehow she's talked you into whatever she wants before you know it."

"That sounds like Celia. It's nice to know it works on everybody, not just me." I replayed the dinner in my head where she'd so skillfully dropped Jasper in my lap, but couldn't bring myself to be mad at her. I looked at him out of the corner of my eye as we reached the steps, and he seemed lost in thought. Mentally steeling myself for the sun again, I held my breath as we began to climb. It wasn't so bad at first, but the longer we climbed, the more the heat angered my skin. When we finally reached our level, I rush-walked the last few steps to cross into the shade.

Relief flooded me, and it once again confirmed that I'd be miserable tomorrow. At least our boat tonight would be covered, so I wouldn't be in the sun the rest of the day. Jasper was eyeing me quizzically, but didn't comment on my weird behavior as he walked me the last few feet. As we stopped in front of my door, warmth flooded me at the memory of the last time we'd stood in this spot.

He slowly slipped my beach bag off his shoulder, and held it out for me to take. Unlike the sweltering kiss last night, today he just brushed an escaped strand of hair aside, and tucked it carefully behind my ear. He leaned down and left a whisper-soft kiss on my lips.

"I won't keep you, since you need to get in that cool shower. But I'll see you for our boat ride, right?"

"Right."

"Okay, then. Let me know if you need anything—I'll be right next door."

"Okay. Thank you." I smiled at him, and his return smile nearly knocked me off my feet. Rather than fall over like an idiot, though, I turned and managed to let myself into the room without incident. *That man is addling my brain more and more by the minute.*

I dropped the sandy beach bag right inside the door, and made a beeline for the shower. Twisting the nozzle to a barely-not-freezing temp, I then struggled for several minutes to extricate myself from my white gauzy cover up without killing my shoulders. When I stepped into the shower, the force of the water stung, despite the chilly temperature. I toughed it out, though, and by the end my skin had numbed a fair bit.

I was gingerly wrapped in a fluffy white towel and pawing through my suitcase for something to wear which didn't require going over my head or touching my shoulders when a brisk knock sounded at the door.

I tightened my towel for good measure, and walked over to check the peephole. It was a woman in the resort uniform, carrying a silver tray. Flipping open the lock, I peered through a crack in the door to hide my towel-clad state.

"Hello, Ms. Anderson?"

"Uhm, yes?"

"We have your order for you!" her chipper pronouncement didn't clear anything up.

"I'm sorry, I didn't actually order anything . . ." I trailed off.

"Oh, it says here it was sent by a Mr. Lewis?"

My eyebrows shot up. Apparently, Jasper had been busy while I'd been showering. "Oh, okay then, thank you." I pulled the door wider, and she passed me the tray. I balanced it with one hand and held my towel tight with the other. "Thank you, just one minute while I grab my wallet so I can give you a tip."

"No ma'am, Mr. Lewis already took care of me. You call us if you need anything else!" She ducked her head once and then trotted off down the hall towards the stairs.

Kicking the door closed with my foot, I turned and carefully set the tray down on our coffee table. I lifted the lid, and tears pricked my eyes when I saw what was underneath. A tall, frosty glass with a lime wedge, a folded note, and a bottle of after-sun lotion. I picked up the glass and sniffed, then took a sip to find a soursop juice slushie, which was insanely delicious after being in the heat all morning. Lifting the note with my other hand, I opened it to find his scrawling handwriting inside.

Daphne,

No need to tough it out on my account. I hope this helps you feel better, but let me know if you need anything else at all.

Yours,

Jasper

I sunk onto the couch, and held the note to my chest for a long moment. Many thoughts swirled through my head as I drank that delicious soursop slushie, but one stood out from the rest. *He's a keeper.*

There were a lot of facets to my personality that were positive. I mean, I could always make somebody laugh, I never met a stranger, and I could plan a particularly amazing vacation at a moment's notice. On the other hand, I had plenty of less-than-stellar qualities, too. Chief among them, stubbornness.

Tonight I was thankful for it, though, as it was the only way I would make it through this boat ride. And I was determined that I would make it, regardless of how awful I felt—not only did I absolutely love glass-bottomed boats, but I had to tell Jasper thank you for his thoughtful delivery this afternoon.

Buoyed by those thoughts, I carefully placed the bikini top back on, wincing when the straps touched the ever-reddening skin next to the safe zone. I adjusted it, and breathed a sigh of relief. Now, I just had to get my dress on, and I was in the clear. I held my breath as the loose, blue dress floated over my shoulders. Thankfully I had packed it. I almost hadn't—since it's not the most flattering—but in the end, I'd chosen comfort over style, and I was so glad that I had something I could wear tonight without scrubbing my tender, burnt skin. I was surprised it hurt so bad, when it still didn't *look* all that red, but my skin had always been sensitive.

Suitably dressed, I exited the bathroom to find Bea sprawled across the couch in a red maxi dress, nearing the end of her book.

"Girl, you get slower by the minute." She snapped the book shut. "But, I love you anyways. You ready to do this thing?"

"Yep, I'm excited."

"Oooh, excited for the fish and coral, or excited for a certain handsome fella?" She tried to wiggle her eyebrows at me, but just ended up making a crazy face which made me laugh.

"Come on, you nut. It can be both. Besides, don't act like you're not just as excited to spend time with George. You two have had quite a bit of alone time the last twenty-four hours. What have you been up to?" I waggled my eyebrows at her suggestively.

She sighed dreamily, and I couldn't help my grin at seeing my friend so happy, especially knowing George was every bit as love-struck.

"Daphne, I know he's your brother so you'll never agree, but he's god-like. I just keep thinking he can't make me any happier, and he turns around and does something to prove me wrong. Like last night—you and Jasper were completely wrapped up in dancing, but my head was pounding from the music. I told George, and he insisted we go somewhere quieter. I was thinking he'd just take me back to my room and call it an early night. Nope! Not him. He got me a soda to go from the waiter, then took me down to the front desk and got me some Advil for my head. Then, we spent over an hour just walking along the beach, enjoying the scenery."

"You won't hear any arguments from me, as long as you're happy." She looped an arm around my middle and gave me a grateful squeeze as we headed out the door, and I couldn't stop my hiss of pain.

Worry took over her face as she asked, "Are you all right? What's wrong?"

I waved her off. "Nothing major, I just got a little too much sun today."

"Do you need to stay in? I can let the guys know we need to relax here for the night," she offered without a hint of reservation.

"No, I'm absolutely fine. It's not my first sunburn, and it probably won't be my last." I waved off her concern, and we let ourselves out into the hallway, where the guys were waiting.

Our boat was prompt and after wading out from the beach, we climbed right aboard the small vessel. It was only the four of us, the captain, the first mate, and two older couples. We putted slowly out further into the water, and the golden rays of sunset paved our way, and for a while my eyes stayed trained on the beautiful ocean and all that we could see beneath the boat.

Eventually though, my eyes were drawn back to Jasper like a magnet. He looked so exquisite that I completely forgot everything else as soon as my eyes landed on him—a five o'clock shadow dusted his jaw, and for a moment my brain got lost down a rabbit trail wondering what it would feel like to kiss him down that alluring line where his jaw met his neck.

"Daphne, how are you feeling this evening?" His rich voice snapped me out of my wandering thoughts, and I blushed at being caught staring and daydreaming. *At least he can't read minds. Awkward.*

"Fine. Thank you for the lotion earlier, it helped a lot. And it was sweet of you."

"You're welcome. I'm glad to hear it." His eyes crinkled with a smile.

"So, burnt again, baby sister?" George asked from my other side.

I snorted. "I am absolutely fine. It is not a big deal. Sheesh," I exaggerated, making him chuckle.

"Uh-huh. You say that now—the second day is always worse," he muttered. "Just don't overdo it the next few days—Dad will skin my hide if I bring you back blistered."

"I am a grown woman, perfectly capable of taking care of myself." I narrowed my eyes at him, to make sure he got the point.

"You know that, and I know that . . . but to Dad, you will forever be five in a butterfly costume, and no amount of protesting will change that."

I chuckled because he was right.

Jasper was grinning from ear to ear, and leaned down to whisper, "Butterfly costume, eh? Sounds darling."

I shook my head at the teasing as the captain stopped the boat. He started pointing out things that were visible beneath the glass floor, so we stopped talking and started looking. I saw a lot of amazing things in that boat, but not one of them was more beautiful than the man sitting next to me.

TWELVE

Lobster

Pain. Searing, radiating torture was ripping through my shoulders. What is happening right now? I woke with a groan, and attempted to move my arms out from under my pillow to stop it, but ended up hissing through my teeth at the motion-induced misery. Stupid, stupid sun! It felt like my skin was trying to melt off. With painstakingly slow movements, I pulled my arms down, and sat up. I gingerly made my way to the bathroom, and crept in to avoid waking Bea.

The fluorescent lighting revealed the issue immediately, my poor skin was so burnt it nearly glowed everywhere it was exposed. I tentatively worked my way through brushing my teeth and was attempting to apply after-sun lotion when Bea stumbled in, yawning and bleary-eyed.

"Hey, girl, how are you up so early? I just need to use the bathroom and then I'm going to crash for at least another hour." She wandered past me, not looking up.

I continued patting the lotion in as gently as possible, wincing every time my hand made contact. When Bea stumbled back by, she washed her hands and finally looked up at me.

"Oh, no! Daphne, that looks awful. Is it blistered?" Her forehead wrinkled in concern.

"I'm not sure, my arms aren't at least." I sighed and set the lotion bottle down. I'd done everything I could without wrinkling any affected skin and hurting myself worse.

"Well, we are definitely staying in today. You and me, girl time," she declared.

"You and George are supposed to go hike through that cave with the underground pool today. You can't miss that—it was your number one activity for this trip. I'll be fine holed up in the room until you get back," I argued, not wanting to ruin their plans.

"George will understand, and I don't want to leave you here alone. I'm going to tell him right now." She spun on her heel, and was gone—completely ignoring my protests as I made my way back to the bed, where I settled against the curved wooden headboard.

Ten minutes later she was back, looking triumphant. "I've got everything settled. You will have company today, and George still gets to go cave-hiking."

"Is Jasper going with him?" I asked, flipping through TV channels absently.

I heard a masculine throat clearing, and my eyes flicked from the screen to where Bea was standing, Jasper at her side. "Actually, I thought I'd stay with you, so Bea and George can still make their plans today. If that's all right with you, of course?" he asked.

"Oh, Jasper! I didn't see you there." My hand flew to my messy morning bun, and I instantly regretted throwing the same floppy dress from yesterday back on.

He raised his eyebrows expectantly, and it finally dawned that he'd asked a question.

"Of course it's fine if you stay, but I don't want you to miss your activity today, either. You're supposed to be going on your Grand Cayman history tour."

He grinned, and the rakish look set my pulse pounding. "I called the concierge downstairs, and explained the situation. They've already pushed it to tomorrow for me. If you're feeling up to it, we can go together. I checked—there's room for two." He sauntered over, and leaned his hip against the edge of the mattress.

I swallowed hard, my eyes traveling up his gorgeous, pajama-clad frame to meet his smoldering brown eyes, and suddenly couldn't remember a single reason to argue against spending the entire day locked in a room with the gorgeous Brit. I hated history, but if it meant spending tomorrow with him too, I'd gladly take a boring tour.

"As long as you won't be missing out," I said breathlessly.

"Spending the day with you could never be missing out."

My heart melted at the sweet words, and I nodded slowly. "Okay then, it's a plan."

"All right! This is going to be an awesome day all around." Bea did a dorky happy dance, and I couldn't help but laugh at my crazy friend's enthusiasm. "If you'll excuse me, I have to put on my adventurin' clothes. George was almost ready." She grabbed a few things from her suitcase and shut herself into the bathroom.

"I need to get some real clothes on myself, and grab a cuppa so we can settle in for the day. Would you like some tea? Or anything? We can order room service—my treat."

"No, I'm good for now, thank you."

He tapped the bed twice, as if that was that. "I'll be back shortly, then. Don't get too lonely while I'm gone." He gave me a long, lingering look that had my knees turning to jelly.

I shook my head at his dry tone, and watched him walk away. I knew he was going to change, but those pajamas clung very nicely to his shoulders and hips, and I had no complaints.

I found myself in breathless anticipation, waiting for Jasper to return. I had decided to settle onto the couch, so we could both see the TV and sit comfortably without navigating the bed. That just seemed like too much, plus it was harder to get in and out without hurting my delicate skin. It wasn't long after Bea left that he turned back up, a mug with a dangling tea bag in one hand, and a frosty glass in the other.

"Here you are," he pressed the cool glass into my hand, despite my protests. "If you don't want it, you can set it aside. I like bringing you things, so I'm afraid you're stuck with it." He gave me a lopsided grin, and I sipped the drink. Soursop juice, our instant favorite.

"Thank you, it's delicious as usual." I swirled my straw through the creamy drink, and pondered for a minute. Something was prickling at the back of my mind, but I couldn't figure out what. It would come to me eventually. "What do you want to watch today? They have pretty much all the channels."

"Shouldn't it be your choice? You're the one who's burnt; it only seems fair."

I cackled at his naivete. "Okay, I'll choose, but remember you said that." I clicked swiftly through the channels, until I found what I wanted.

He watched for a minute, and a confused frown marred his handsome face. "What is this?"

"Don't tell me you've never watched Anthony Bourdain. He has like eighty-seven shows and they're all good." I waved theatrically at the television.

"No, I can't say that I've heard of him. Honestly, when you laughed over getting to choose I thought you'd force me to sit through the standard chick flick, not this . . . What is that he's eating right now? It looks foul."

"Or fowl, perhaps?" I quipped, and he groaned.

"Har-dee-har. Yes, foul fowl. But the question still stands. That is not recognizable as food." He took a long sip of his tea, and watched with rapt horror as a diminutive local woman fed Anthony something out of a large, simmering pot.

I didn't answer, just settled in next to him and took in the show. It took a few minutes of shifting, but eventually I got the lone pillow arranged in such a way that nothing hurt, and sighed in relief. After a few minutes, I realized that the edge of my thigh was pressed squarely against Jasper's, and the over-thinking ensued in full force.

Should I move? Oh my goodness, I just sighed loudly when I got comfortable, right after I pressed up against him. That's mortifying. Although, he didn't say anything. Maybe he didn't notice? SHOULDN'T he notice when a woman presses her leg against his?

I shifted a little, peeking at him from the corner of my eye to gauge his reaction. He was still enraptured with the show, where the woman was explaining that some of the pots were constantly replenished, never emptied or cleaned.

His eyebrows shot up, and he sipped his tea again. No sign of notice of the leg situation. I shifted again, having gotten myself out of the original, comfort-able position with my last move. I was wriggling around like a puppy needing to pee when his hand rested gently on my leg.

"Are you okay? I can move if you're uncomfortable." His concerned gaze made me blush, and his warm hand was sending a delicious warmth radiating up from my knee, which didn't help at all.

"I'm fine, sorry. You can go back to watching." I bit my lip, and his eyes tracked the movement. He set the cup of tea down, turned so he was facing me, and leaned his elbow on the back of the couch.

"Is he going to keep traveling all over the world, eating questionably disgusting things for the rest of the hour?"

"All of the things don't look as disgusting as geoduck, but yes."

"I see. I'm not sure if it's better or worse that you knew what it was." He tapped his fingers on his knee thoughtfully. "In that case, how about we just talk instead? You can go back to making me watch that poor man eat horrifying foods later."

"O-kay . . . what do you want to talk about?" I muted the TV, and shimmied around so I was facing him, as well.

"I dunno, we can talk about anything. I just want to know more about you."

I shrugged one shoulder out of habit, and then winced. "There's not much more to know, really. I think we've covered the highlights. But you can ask me anything you want, so long as I can ask you the same questions."

"That seems fair enough. Where to begin? Ahh, how about an easy one—what's your dream travel destination?"

"Easy? You just asked a travel agent what my dream destination is, as if there's only one!" He grinned, but didn't change the question. "Okay, okay. If I can really only pick one, it would have to be Norway."

He seemed completely surprised by my answer. "Norway? What is there to see in Norway?"

"Well, on the surface it seems like a small country, without a whole lot of tourist draws beyond the typical mountains and whatnot. However"—I pointed my finger to punctuate my thought—"that would be a wrong assumption. There are reindeer farms, there are the northern lights, and, coolest of all, there are glass igloos you can stay in."

"Glass igloos? That sounds counter intuitive. Wouldn't you be cold in one of those in the winter?"

"Nah, they're heated. And they have giant, comfy beds with tons of blankets. But that's not the point. The point is that you can lay in that cozy bed at night, and stare through the glass dome and see the northern lights."

"Ahh, I see. Well, that does sound enchanting, with the right person."

"Now you're catching on. What about you? Didn't you say your dream destination was Australia?"

"Well, almost. I do want to see Australia. But, my absolute dream is New Zealand."

"It's a beautiful country, for sure. What drew you to it? Was it just work?" I remembered him saying it was his dream job.

He covered his face with his palm in embarrassment. "You're going to laugh."

I scrunched my eyebrows together at his reaction, now even more determined to hear the story. "Uh, too bad. A deal's a deal."

He threw his head back. "I saw it on Lord of the Rings."

A tiny chuckle squeaked out of me, despite my best efforts to contain it.

"Ah-ah, no laughing! It's a perfectly acceptable movie."

"I'm not laughing, laughing. It's kind of cute! So, you're a Lord of the Rings nerd?"

"If appreciating an excellent story line makes me a nerd, then so be it. I accept the title with dignity." He gave a little exaggerated bow.

That made me laugh for real. When I could finally breathe again, I had to ask, "So, you want to go to New Zealand to find Frodo?"

"No! I mean, they do apparently have hobbit homes there you can tour, but that's not the point. It was the most beautiful place I'd ever seen, in real life or in film. The views are stunning, the land has this drama to it that you just don't see everywhere. Sweeping vistas, stark drops, sudden changes in landscape . . . It's visually unique and, as an architectural engineer, that really speaks to me. I've always had this vision of one day getting to go there, and help create magnificent structures in this enchanting place. The idea that my work could improve a place like that, well . . . it's a heady thought, honestly."

No longer laughing, I thought over his answer. "It does make sense, the land is beautiful. It's just cute that you're so embarrassed about liking a movie." I leaned over and booped him on the nose with my finger.

His jaw dropped. "Did you just bop me on the nose like some kind of cat?"

My answering smile was so wide, my cheeks hurt.

"Oh, my lovely girl, you are lucky that sunburn is protecting you right now, because otherwise I might feel the uncontrollable urge to tickle you." He tried to look menacing, but failed miserably.

"Next question!" I sing-songed.

He narrowed his eyes, but thought it over. "Okay, I'd love to know how you found out about your health conditions. You said there were two? That doesn't seem like the sort of thing most young women know, before trying to have kids. I know men certainly don't get their fertility checked out."

"Ahh," I said, and fear soured my stomach. Here we go, straight to the nitty gritty. "Well, it's probably not a super fun conversation, but I will tell you if you really want . . ." I grimaced, but he didn't look put off. He nodded for me to continue.

"Okay, well, when I was fifteen, I started having a lot of pain every month with my cycle. Like, intense, crippling, double-over-and-don't-breathe sort of pain. The first month, we assumed it was just a bad month. A fluke, or something. The second month, it was so bad I couldn't go to school for two days and, well, my parents were really worried."

"Understandably so, you were young, and that sounds terrible." Genuine concern laced his words, and I didn't hear any discomfort at the topic, so I soldiered on with the unpleasant memories.

"Yeah, it was. So, we went to the doctor, and at first they brushed it off—they told me to take tylenol and try a heating pad." I scoffed in annoyance at the memory. "I'd practically lived on a heating pad both times it had happened, so it felt like he wasn't even listening to me. The third month rolled around, just the same. My mom was livid that the doctor hadn't even bothered to try and help, so she scheduled me for an appointment with another doctor on the other side of town. That one took us seriously, and scheduled some tests. Long story short, I have both endometriosis, and PCOS. The intense pain was caused by ovarian cysts." I trailed off, unsure what else to say.

"Wow, I'm so sorry. That sounds like a terrible way to get that news. And at fifteen . . . well, it just proves what I already suspected: that you're an incredibly strong woman. To have gone through that, and come out on the other side of it is impressive. But I wish you hadn't had to endure it." He reached over and laced his fingers with mine, and that small, unexpected touch made me feel better about the painful memories.

I'd always been afraid to share them, but it felt right with him. And he hadn't been anything but kind about it, which was a relief.

"Thank you," I murmured as I searched his face.

He squeezed my fingers gently, and I thought he was going to kiss me. Instead, he prompted, "It's your turn to ask the next question."

Hmm, what to ask? A knock at the door saved me from having to think something else up.

"Oh, good, that should be breakfast." He hopped up, and strode across the room to answer.

"We didn't order breakfast!"

"Yes, I did. That's what took me so long when I got tea. Besides, did you really think I wouldn't feed you all day?"

By then, he'd opened the door and let in the yellow-clad delivery man. He pushed in an overloaded tray of silver domes, and all the familiar scents of breakfast washed over me. My stomach growled in anticipation. Jasper signed the bill with a flourish, and passed it back to him. He gave us a little half-bow, and left us to enjoy our meal.

Jasper started lifting and setting aside the domes, revealing a breakfast feast of epic proportions. We couldn't eat it all if we tried, and it must have cost a fortune.

"You did not need to do all this! You are spoiling me," I exclaimed as he handed me a plate loaded with a giant, fluffy waffle topped with strawberry butter and powdered sugar . . . because vacation.

"Maybe I like spoiling you," he said without a hint of shame. "You don't seem to let many people get that close, so I'll consider it an honor." I took a huge bite of my waffle as he raised his glass of ice water, and nodded for me to pick up my glass, too. Once I did, he proposed a toast. "To excellent breakfast companions."

"To excellent breakfast companions," I concurred, clinking the rim of my glass to his. I then took a hearty chug to wash down my waffle. Water spilled down the side of my lip, and before I could stop it, he quickly caught it with the side of his thumb. I froze, embarrassed by the spill, but quickly caught up in his heated gaze. He ran his thumb under my lip again, and my lips parted of their own accord.

Without wasting another second, he leaned forward and claimed my lips in a kiss just as decadent as the sugary waffle had been. His fingertips threaded gently into my hair, and I leaned in closer, wanting every little bit of him. I abandoned my glass on the side table, and rested my cold fingertips on his shoulder, where his firm muscles joined his neck. He was solid, and warm, and everything I wanted to get lost in.

After a few glorious moments we pulled apart. The heat in his eyes hadn't dimmed one bit, and I knew mine were the same. No matter how many kisses we shared, I couldn't seem to get enough of this man. It was shaping up to be a long day, in the best possible sort of way.

The day wore on, filled with little touches and an endless stream of movies after we'd given up on travel shows. Despite my burnt skin preventing any real cuddling, it felt like an enchanted afternoon to have so much uninterrupted time with him. We'd known each other for a few months, yes, but most of that time was in passing, or in the company of other people. Nothing like this, where we could talk and laugh and just be.

My mind was floating happily, head leaned against his firm shoulder, watching an action movie I'd never seen before and sipping on my second soursop juice of the day, when an idea hit me.

"Oh my gosh!" I sat bolt upright, startling Jasper and nearly spilling my delicious nectar-of-the-gods.

"What is it? Are you okay?" He looked me up and down, searching for the cause of my outburst.

"Yes, I'm fine! I figured out how to help the Judes!" I flapped my free hand with excitement.

"That's great! How?"

I grabbed his arm. "It's actually simple. They wanted to try something new, something fun. Totally reasonable. But, things went south when they messed with a town staple. Everybody loves their sweet tea. It's a sacred cow, if you will. You can't go tipping those, or people get upset. However, the idea of bringing some pizzazz to the menu is sound. Well, they need to make this." I held up the glass of delicious juice, and his forehead wrinkled.

"Well, yes, I'm sure the people back home would love it as much as we do, but . . . didn't you say on the first day that soursop is native to this area? I doubt it's easy to get back home, and probably quite expensive."

"Yeah, I'm sure it is. But peaches aren't. They're plentiful, and sweet, and would be divine mixed up in whatever else is in here with the juice, instead of in some instant tea." I eyed the glass, not having the foggiest idea what else was in there.

He thought intently for a moment, and stared at the glass right along with me. "I think you're onto something, but how do we find out what else it's made with? Bea might be able to guess something close, but, if we don't get it right, it may just be a disappointment."

"You're right, and that's not what they need after the Dolly-induced dry spell they've been having."

I flopped back against the couch, and groaned when my back made contact. Stupid burnt pale skin.

Jasper winced in sympathy. "Can I rub some more of the sun lotion on for you? It should help with the sting."

"Sure, let me get it."

"Let me. You get as comfortable as you can, and pull your hair aside so it doesn't get sticky," he ordered, and crossed to the side table where the tube of sun lotion was waiting.

I did as he asked, still pondering the issue of the potential peach juice—or PPJ, as I was calling it in my head. "I bet there are at least a few recipes online."

He perched behind me on the couch, and carefully smoothed the lotion over my shoulders. I felt a whisper of a touch as he shifted the shoulder of my dress over, and then applied more to the skin there.

My mind blanked out for a moment, distracted by his soothing touch. He was tall, and strong, and could probably toss me over his shoulder if he wanted, yet he was treating me as if I was a fragile baby bird. It was nice in a way I didn't even know I'd wanted.

"There probably are several variations, but how will we know if they're good or not?"

Warmth spread through my chest at his casual use of we, as if we were in this together.

"Well, we'd have to test them out, and frankly I can't cook to save my life. I mean, you probably just blend it all up, right?"

"I don't know, it's awfully smooth. Blended things tend to be a bit chunkier. Maybe they've sieved it?"

"That sounds complicated. I wish we could just ask for the recipe," I murmured, as Jasper carefully fixed the shoulders of my dress and then moved to the other side.

"Technically, you could. They might say no, or they might be willing to share. There's only one way to find out," he pointed out helpfully.

We sat in silence as he finished lotioning me up, and then he stepped away to wash the rest of the lotion from his hands.

"Thank you, that is feeling much better," I said when he returned and took his spot next to me on the couch. "Although, I hope you know you didn't have to."

He shook his head, looking amused. "Daphne, I must not be making myself clear enough. So let me try it straight—I enjoy taking care of you. You're this incredibly strong, independent woman, and I admire that. But, it's okay to be soft at times, too. To let someone in who wants to help you; care for you. It doesn't make you any less strong, or any less amazing."

I rolled my eyes, but appreciated the sentiment. He leaned forward again, and I leaned in as well, ready for his kiss. Instead, I got a boop on the nose.

"Hey, really?" I complained, and this time he was the one laughing.

"Fair is fair." He gestured with the remote. "You should call down to the front desk and see about that recipe. Maybe you can work your travel agent magic."

Well, when he put it that way, I couldn't very well say no.

THIRTEEN

Crashing in the Moonlight

The last day of our trip passed in a blur. The four of us just hung out around the resort, and talked. Dreaming about future trips, and all the places we'd like to see. After pedicures, we made it back down to the beach, where the ladies camped under a shady pavilion to watch the men play volleyball with some other resort guests. As the bright Caribbean sun faded into night, I felt that familiar feeling of never wanting the trip to end. I felt so much closer to Jasper, and I was starting to worry that being back home would change things.

Could we still be in our little new relationship bubble once we were surrounded by all of our normal life responsibilities? I didn't know, and the worry pricked at my thoughts throughout the day. Tonight, I was pulling out all the stops. We might be going home tomorrow, but we had one last night in paradise, and I wanted to make sure he never forgot the time we spent together here. I looked in the mirror, trying to decide if I needed to change anything. My gown for the evening was floor-length, and grecian in style. The fabric was white, but with a pearlescent overlay that gleamed as the light hit it just so with my movements. Subtle, yet beautiful. The neckline was ruched and twisted into a sleeveless style, and the empire waistline was embedded with tiny, sparkling beads that were fit for a princess.

I'd done my hair swept up off my neck in a casual twisted up-do, and had a white-gold rope necklace which paired nicely with the overall style. Thankfully the sunburn had soaked in a lot over the past twenty-four hours, so I was no longer glowing. Overall, I think the effect was what I was going for. If this didn't knock him off his feet, well, I didn't know what would. Satisfied, I slipped on my white flip-flops, and settled them under the hem of the gown.

Bea stuck her head out of the closet. "Can I get your opinion on this dress? I liked it at home, but I'm just not sure."

"Of course, let's see it."

She stepped out, and I could see that she'd gone all out as well. "It's perfect," I said, and I meant it. Her dress—unlike mine—cut off just above the knees, and was a vibrant red. With her ebony hair and fresh tan, she looked like she belonged on a runway, not a moonlit beach for a buffet.

"Okay, good. I know it's fancy, but I just fell in love with it." She smoothed her hand over the side of the dress, fixing an invisible wrinkle. "Do you think George will like it?"

"Without a doubt. We'll be lucky if he doesn't swallow his tongue and have to go to the clinic, instead of dinner."

She laughed, and took me in from head to toe. "Well, Jasper isn't going to be any better when he sees you. Speaking of, things seem to be going pretty well for you two on this trip." She raised one eyebrow in question.

I couldn't help the stupid grin that spread across my face, and I perched on the edge of the bed. "It's better than good, honestly. I feel like I'm dreaming. He's everything I've ever wanted in a man, and I want to pinch myself that he wants me, too. He's intelligent, and kind, and so thoughtful. I just—what if he changes his mind, Bea? How do I get over that fear? Because, it's so strong. I've only known him for a few months, we've only started to scratch the surface of more for a few days, and I'm so deep in my feelings for him. I've never let myself feel like this for anyone, and it's terrifying." The rushing tumble of words stopped, and I stared down at my hands.

She sat across from me on the edge of her bed and crossed her arms. "I don't think you can make yourself get over it—not really. You just have to decide that he's worth the risk. Are you better off for being in a relationship with him?"

I picked at one of my fingernails anxiously. "We're not even officially in a relationship, really. I mean, I feel like we're dating. Sort of? We're on this amazing trip together, we've spent every waking moment together for a few days, so it's kind of on overdrive. But he hasn't officially asked me to be his girlfriend, so nothing's official official. But, yes, I think he brings out the best in me. The brave in me." I thought about having shared my medical issues—and the fears they caused—with him, something I'd never told anyone before, not even Bea.

"Then it sounds like you've already decided., she said simply.

Could it be that simple? Could I just be all in, and let what happened happen? I let out a long exhale, thinking it over. There wasn't much choice. My heart had already decided, despite the risks. I was in love with Jasper, and denying it wouldn't change a thing.

Bea's phone buzzed, and she picked it up and read a text. "The guys got us a great table, right next to the water. Are you ready to head down?"

I nodded, and she fired off a quick return text before abandoning the phone to the side table.

"Let's go knock their socks off!" She grinned at me, and I grinned back. I didn't have the heart to tell her they probably weren't wearing any socks, due to the sand. We could knock their metaphorical socks off, at least.

The beach was magical, bathed in the moonlight. Tiki torches surrounded a temporary dance floor on the sand; a huge buffet had been hauled out on one side and insanely delicious smells of roasted meat and caramelized onions were permeating the air; and I could see Jasper, standing with his hip propped against a table at the far end of the throngs of resort-goers, scanning the crowd. When his eyes landed on me, they lit up and I felt my heart skip in response. I could never get enough of this feeling, if I lived to be a hundred and eighty years old.

I dodged through the merry crowd, and wound my way to his side.

"Hey, handsome." I winked at him.

"Hey, yourself, gorgeous." He leaned down and pressed a kiss to my cheek, and—forget the warm night—his kiss was what brought a flush burning to my cheeks. The brief touch wasn't nearly enough, but we were surrounded by people, and George was talking to us. Maybe later we can steal a few more kisses.

"Do you want to dance first, or eat first? I'm good either way," George half-hollered, to be heard over the pounding drums.

"I'm up for whatever," Jasper responded.

"We'll eat later, let's get out there and dance!" Bea voted.

"What she said," I agreed.

"We have to give the ladies what they want." Jasper grinned at me as he took my hand and made a bee-line for the dance floor. In no time at all, we were lost to the rhythm.

Something about Jasper just made time pass strangely. Away from him, life went in slow motion.

It dragged on like it had weights tied to its sad, arthritic ankles. With him? It was like everything around us was on speed, zooming past while we were in our private bubble. What felt like five minutes of dancing in his arms turned out to be nearly an hour, and Bea finally dragged us to the buffet to stuff our faces in preparation for dancing, round two.

The food was delicious, and we laughed about everything and nothing while we chowed down. I crossed my legs under the table, and my foot connected with Jasper's knee. He jumped, and I reached out and grabbed his arm.

"Sorry, didn't mean to kick you!"

He chuckled. "I see how it is, you're feeling impatient so you start beating me up, now?" He shook his head and tsked in mock disappointment.

"Nope, just having a Bea moment."

"A Bea moment?" He looked confused, and it was adorable.

"Yes, Bea is good at so many things, but she is as clumsy as they come. I think we've been friends so long, she's rubbing off on me."

"Hey! I heard that." She pointed her fork at me menacingly.

I shrugged. "If the shoe fits, try not to trip over it."

She stuck her tongue out at me, but didn't deny her clumsiness. I blew her a kiss, and she blew me one in return.

Our lighthearted banter resumed, but my foot had somehow found its way behind Jasper's knee, and I trailed it lightly up and down the back of his calf. The tiny bit of contact was distracting, and I didn't hear a word of whatever George said next. I also completely missed the resort employee approaching our table, so I was shocked when he addressed Jasper.

"Excuse me, Mr. Lewis?"

"Yes?"

"We have an urgent call for you in the office. If you'll follow me, I'll take you to it." The yellow-clad man bobbed his head and then, gesturing with both arms, indicated the path away from the beach party in full swing.

"Do you want me to come?" I asked, worried about this phone call. Everyone knew we were on vacation, so it must be something important, and my mind immediately jumped to the worst-case scenario.

"No, it's probably just mum asking about a phone tour of the Caymans. You stay and dance—I'll be back in no time." He gave my hand a quick squeeze, and followed the employee off through the crowd.

A lump formed in my stomach, and I completely lost my appetite. Somehow I didn't think his mom would be expecting a phone tour from the office landline. I watched with growing dread until his back was out of sight.

The next half hour passed with excruciating slowness as Bea and George danced while I watched from our table, fiddling with the tablecloth hem. They asked me to join them, but the dancing mood had flown right out of me when I watched my dance partner walk away. When I finally saw Jasper coming back towards us with a dazed expression, my worry reached its breaking point. George spotted him also, and pulled a loved-up Bea from the dance floor to see what was up.

Nerves choking me, George beat me to the question. "Everything okay back home, man?"

"Yes, actually. It was good news." He shook his head slowly, his bewildered expression giving nothing away.

George chuckled. "Are you sure about that?"

"Yes, I'm just in shock. Please, don't hold up the evening on my account," he insisted.

"Well, in that case, Bea and I are going to go for one last moonlit stroll before we leave tomorrow. That is, if you're good, Daph?" George looked at me with a strange expression on his face, but I couldn't decipher it. I waved them on, too in knots over what Jasper was going to say to worry about George and Bea going for a walk.

He seemed to hum with nervous energy as he guided Bea away, his hand on the small of her back. I let them drop out of my mind as Jasper sunk into his seat next to mine, and found my voice. "So, what was the call about?" I hated how anxious I sounded, so I added quickly and with forced excitement, "Good news?"

Jasper ran a hand through his hair, and blew out a breath. "I got offered a new position. I still can't even believe it, honestly. I haven't been on this assignment that long, but apparently the head of the firm sang my praises on the last check-in with my company, and they took it to account. Well, a vacancy opened up, and they offered me the new position, and that's why they called. They want me to meet the client within twenty-four hours of our return tomorrow." He paused and took a slow draw from his umbrella-topped drink.

"Oh, really? Where is the new job?" My voice came out small, strained. Please don't be far, please don't be far.

"Ahh." His face fell, and in that moment I knew it was bad. For me, anyway. "It's New Zealand. They offered me my dream spot in New Zealand. Apparently, one of the current architectural engineers is retiring early to his family's farm up in Canada."

My heart crumbled into dust, dry as the Sahara and blown away as quickly as the sand that lived there. I forced myself to swallow—an impressive feat with the heart dried up and blown out of my chest like that. "Congratulations, Jasper. I'm so pleased for you."

He searched my eyes, as if trying to discern my sincerity. I'm sure the words sounded hollow, because hollowness was all that was left inside of me.

"We should call it a night, then. Sounds like you'll be extremely busy the next couple of days." I slid my chair back and stood in a fluid motion, intent on escaping him before I broke into a million pieces.

"Daphne," he said in a whisper, but I didn't stop. I just walked away from the table, brushing past all the happy, vacationing people. To think, I'd been one of them before Jasper dropped his news.

I could feel him hot on my heels. Despite the throng of dancers I was weaving through, he was like a homing beacon at my back calling out for me to turn, and throw myself into his arms. But I wouldn't do that, because I was stronger than the urge. I had an iron will, a fierce strength built over years of holding myself and my expectations for love tightly in hand.

"Daphne!" he called again, a little louder, as if I hadn't heard him over the music the first time. Still, I pressed on, out of the sweaty bodies, through the fine sugar-sand, and up the first few steps towards our rooms before his hand snaked out and caught my arm.

"Daphne, wait. We need to talk about this." His eyebrows were scrunched together with a tense line in the middle.

"There's not really much else to talk about, is there? We go home tomorrow, and you'll be packing up to head to New Zealand the next day." I punctuated the timeline with my hands—I could never seem to keep my hands still when I was upset.

He ground his teeth together, jaw pulsing in protest. "It's not that simple. You and I—"

"You and I have had a lovely vacation, and I will always remember it fondly." That was a lie. I'd always remember it with a stab of pain to my non-existent heart. Because, truly, his memories would cut me deep for a long, long time. There was no other way for me to process how hard and fast I'd fallen. I spun on my heel and made it up three more steps before his words wrapped around me again.

"Would you stop, for God's sake!" he yelled, and I froze in shock. "I'm sorry for shouting, truly, but you just keep running off and leaving me when I'm trying to talk to you." His feet pounded up the steps and he stopped just above me, as if his physical presence on the next stair would keep me where he wanted me.

"What is it you want me to say, Jasper?"

"I don't know, but we can't just leave it like this—you running off mad, and me leaving the country!"

He was actually exasperated, and the depth of his feelings cut me another inch deeper. "You've got to be kidding me! I'm trying to let you go gracefully, Jasper—surely you can see that? What do you want from me—to throw myself on you and sob? Well, I'm not that kind of girl. We Southerners have a bit more of a game face than that, so I'm sorry to disappoint." I crossed my arms, my temper rising to fill the empty void of emotion.

"I don't understand. You're angry with me, when you won't have an adult conversation about this?"

I snorted. "What's left to discuss? We've had a great time, and now you're leaving. There's nothing to be said except 'have a safe trip.'"

"That's how you feel?" His eyes glinted in the moonlight, and the picture of him framed there would haunt me for the rest of my days.

"Yes, that's how I feel."

"Then, you're right. I guess there is nothing else to discuss, after all." His face shuttered, and he stepped aside and gestured up the stairs, allowing me to pass.

I set my shoulders and walked by. Don't look back, don't look back, don't look back.

I made it all the way to my room without crumbling. When the door clicked shut behind me and the darkness surrounded me, I pressed my back against the door, and slid down to the cold, hard tile floor. The tears started as a trickle, but there in the privacy of my room the racking sobs finally broke free.

Some time later, I was curled in bed with my back towards the door, soggy covers clenched in my fist when I heard the lock open, and Bea's timid steps inside. She tiptoed across the room and turned on a single bedside lamp.

"Daph?" she whispered, testing to see if I was awake, but didn't come closer. I stared out the window at the fat, low moon, but didn't answer her hopeful query.

"I have something to tell you, if you're awake." I barely breathed, trying to hold still so she'd assume I was asleep. It probably made me a bad friend, but I just couldn't take any more change that night. Tomorrow I'd suck it up.

After a moment, she tiptoed to the bathroom, and I heard her shower, change, and tiptoe back to bed. Once the light clicked off again, my shoulders relaxed. Eventually, her breathing evened out and I once again stared at the moon, alone with the silent tears trailing down my stinging cheeks.

Fourteen

Roost

Somewhere around four a.m. I'd given up on the idea of sleep. So, as quietly as humanly possible, I packed all of my things into my suitcase, propped it by the door, and let myself out to walk the beach alone. I walked, letting the wind whip my face and the cool night breeze pebble the skin on my arms, until the sun was fully over the horizon. Then, I turned around and made the long trek back.

When I let myself back into our room, Bea was perched on the edge of her bed, an apprehensive look on her face and her packed suitcase for company.

"Daphne! I was getting worried. But, I'm glad you're back. I have something to tell you, and then we have to get going to the airport!"

"Sorry, I just wanted one last beach walk before we left," I mumbled. "What's up?" I tapped my key card on my suitcase handle distractedly.

"Uhm, well, George proposed last night!" She held up her left hand, and a lovely diamond winked up at me.

"Oh, Bea, congratulations!" I walked over and took her hand, examining the ring. "It's beautiful, really. I'm so happy for you both. You're perfect for each other." I looked up from the ring to the happiness and love shining in her eyes, and despite the flicker of happiness trying to burn for her in my chest, I broke down into sobs again.

"What? I— Oh my!" Bea jumped to her feet and wrapped me in a hug. "I thought you'd be happy, I—"

"I am. I'm so sorry. I'm really happy, it's just—" I choked out, and then sobbed some more.

"Shh, it's okay, you can tell me in a minute." She patted me slowly on the back, and eventually the words came out in a long, tangled tumble. By the end, she was crying with me. Because that's what best friends do.

The ride to the airport was silent. After we'd finished our cry fest, Bea had excused herself for a moment—presumably to explain the situation to George, who'd offered me a hug when it was time to leave, but didn't pry. Jasper had stood off to the side, not angry but certainly aloof. It stung, either way.

After that it was just moving point A to point B. The van dropped us off at the teaspoon-sized airport, and we shuffled inside to check our bags and wait at our gate. I made myself as scarce as possible with so few shop options, and only turned up precisely on time to board the flight. I then claimed the window seat furthest from Jasper.

Bea had slid into the best-friend-buffer position with the ferocity of a pissed-off mother badger, and stayed pointedly between me and any awkward moments at all times. The sleepless night was dragging at me by the time we lifted off, but my gritty eyes refused to shut and let my vulnerability show. Instead I stared out the window with my forehead pressed against it and my angry girl music turned up loud.

Eventually Bea pressed a sprite into my hand, and I thanked her and sipped it without turning away from the window or taking off my headphones. The empty can disappeared in the same manner, and countless sad songs later I watched the ground get closer as we came in to land. Touchdown—usually the moment that caused my stomach to tense at the bump-bump of wheels meeting pavement—elicited a sigh of relief. We were so close to separation.

Sometime in the night, my mind had shifted away from the pain of being apart from Jasper—separated by the whole bulk of the planet between our two specs of earth—and into self-preservation mode. And self-preservation mode demanded that I get away from him, immediately, to lick my wounds in private. Because, boy, did I have wounds. I'd kept myself closed off for so long from the possibility of love, that, when I finally opened that gate a tiny crack, a flood of emotion had come through and latched onto Jasper. That was the only reasonable explanation for why I'd fallen so hard so fast, surely. Enough time would pass eventually that I'd gain perspective on the whole thing. I hope.

Typically a patient person, right then it felt like anxiety was trying to claw its way up and out my throat as I watched people offload from the plane so. freaking. slowly. Truly, it was almost an art form how humanity had managed to make something so simple become so painful. When it was our turn, it took all of my will power not to bolt from the plane at a dead run. Bea let me go first, and I crushed down the desire to run, and led the way at a brisk walk. Off the plane. Past the luggage pickup carousels where we snagged our suitcases. Straight to the idling delivery SUV where Celia waited.

She instantly spotted the diamond glittering on Bea's finger, and thankfully that drew all the attention away from my sullen expression, and Jasper's screaming silence. We bumped down the cobblestone main street to the Sweet Nothings Bake Shop, and I practically leapt from the car as soon as it was in park.

"My, my," Celia said blandly as I hauled my luggage from the back. "You seem antsy as a long-tailed cat in a rocking chair factory. What has got you in such a snit?" Her voice lowered on the last question, so as not to be overheard by the rest of our party.

Apparently not all of her attention was on Bea and George, after all. "Nothing, Celia. Just tired from the trip."

"I see." She pursed her lips and lifted one eyebrow, the perfect arch judging my statement without a word. "Well, you can come on back and tell me about it once you're unpacked."

The statement was posed as a friendly suggestion, but I knew she'd hunt me down if I didn't. With a sigh, I nodded and bolted around the back to where Bert—trusty old Bert—was waiting for me. I was just pulling out of the lot when George and Bea made it to the back lot to leave, themselves. She gave me a sad nod, and he lifted one hand in a wave, concern etched into his usually jovial features.

One terse nod in acknowledgement later, I cranked down the window, turned the country station all the way up, and let the wind lash the tears away from my eyes as I headed out of town. The sight of my little yellow house—just as I'd left it—unleashed something inside of me.

All the bravado and last burst of energy which had carried me home ran out of me in a whoosh as I stumbled through the door. I abandoned my suitcase right inside the door, flipped the lock, padded through the house, abandoning shoes mid-stride, and dumping my purse on the kitchen counter. My bed greeted me like an old friend, and I collapsed into it with gusto. From one heartbeat to the next, my sandpaper eyes closed, and I slept.

The quick double beep of a horn roused me as the waning evening sunlight shone through my bedroom window. With a groan, I pushed myself upright, and moved to the front door with all the speed of a geriatric sloth. A happy bark and whuffling sounds under the front door got me to move a bit quicker, though, once I realized who was here.

I swung the door wide, and Barcelona practically flew up and into my arms, his long ears flapping like undersized wings.

"Barc! Oh, bubba, I missed you, sweet dog!" I squeezed him in a hug, and then turned and waved to my parents, where they waited by the gate. "Hey, Mom! Hey, Dad! Are you coming in?"

"Oh, no sweetie! George called earlier and told us you were exhausted and sunburnt. We are going out for dinner with the Klines, but we can swing back by with something for you, if you want? Then maybe we can catch up on Sunday, for lunch after church?"

"I can't wait to see the pictures!" my dad added with a smile.

Thank God for helpful older brothers. "Dinner would be great, and yes to Sunday. I just need a hug first." I let Barc slide back to the ground, and he dutifully plastered himself to my leg as we crossed the yard. I threw my arms wide and enveloped them both, and the epic group hug was a balm to my aching heart. With one last squeeze, they released me. Dad planted a kiss on my forehead, and Mom ran her hand gently over my hair. Then, with promises to drop back by with delicious takeout for me, they headed off.

Barc's entire body wagged as we headed in to the foyer, and I dropped down on my haunches to give him some more scratches behind the ears. "You're my good boy, aren't you? You wouldn't leave Mama, that's for sure." Sadness pierced me yet again, and I choked back a sob as the situation with Jasper surged back to the forefront of my mind.

Barc just licked my nose, and his tail thumped the floor. With one final scratch, I stood back up and headed for the shower. I had to wash the awful ending to that trip off of me, and then it was back to bed, but with Barc for company this time.

I spent the next day on the couch, wearing too-big sweats, a ratty t-shirt splattered with paint, and big fuzzy socks. Barc highly approved of my couch potato plans, so I pretended it was for him. My brain just wouldn't stop obsessing over how things had gone down with Jasper, and regret was causing the start of what I was sure would be a massive headache. I hated that our last exchange was so angry, but I didn't know what to do about it. He was leaving, but I was never leaving Adele—at least not for long. It was a recipe for a breakup.

I sighed, blowing a strand of frizzy hair from my face. It just wasn't meant to be. I knew it from the start, so why does it hurt so badly?

Several hours into my "Parenthood" marathon, a brisk knock came from the front door. Barc's ears perked up, and he yipped once before trotting over to investigate. With a weary sigh, I hauled myself from the couch to see who it was. Probably Tracy, my neighbor to see how the trip had gone. She was nice like that, but I really didn't want to talk about it yet.

Barc sat to the side of the door, eagerly pressing his nose to the crack and trying to snort the smell through a half-second sooner. Nudging him aside with my foot, I pulled the door open. "Hey, Tracy—" I stopped mid-sentence, because my neighbor was not at the door.

"Hello, Daphne." His velvety, proper voice washed over me, and sent a shiver down my spine with those two little words.

"Hey, Jasper," I answered, and quickly ran my fingers through my snarled hair in embarrassment. "Uhm, I wasn't expecting you, not after . . ."

"I know, but I couldn't just leave things the way they were yesterday. Can we sit?" He gestured to my wooden porch swing.

"Yeah, of course." I pulled the door shut, and followed him the short distance down the porch. I sunk onto the familiar seat, and he settled next to me.

The silence stretched between us, filled with tension. A thousand things to say poured through my head, but since he'd sought me out, it seemed only fair to let him say what he came here to say. Without running scared, like the first time.

"I don't want to just give up on us," he stated calmly and rationally. "You and I, we're so good together. I've never felt this strongly about anyone else, Daphne. I don't say that lightly. I really . . ." He cleared his throat, and seemed unsure. I reached over and squeezed his hand. He looked down in surprise, and then his eyes flickered up and locked with mine.

"I'm falling in love with you, Daphne. I can't just walk away from you, from us, and not at least tell you that."

My heart froze in my chest at his words. He was falling in love with me, too? In an instant, I was flying higher than the highest cloud, lit with joy at the revelation. The moment of elation didn't last, however. The cruel reality was that he was still leaving. I looked over his shoulder to where his sleek, shiny sports car was parked next to Bert. Yet another way we were nothing alike. His suitcases were probably already in the trunk, and the thought sent a tear rolling down my cheek.

"Jasper, I'm selfishly glad to hear you say that, because I'm falling in love with you, too." I took a fortifying breath. "But, it doesn't change anything. You're still going to New Zealand, and I'm still going to be here, in Adele, Georgia, without you. The whole fat world between us."

His eyebrows hitched at me calling the world fat, but when there was that much separation between you and the one man you cared about, it felt fat.

"What if I don't go? My contract here still had another seven weeks left. Loads more time."

I squeezed his hand, hating the words that had to come out of my mouth next. "Jasper, I would love nothing more than for you to stay. But in seven weeks, we'd just be having this conversation all over again. And it would hurt worse, because we'd be more attached."

"Maybe not; maybe we could work something out. Long distance relationships work for some people, right?" His voice was flat, despite the question.

I leaned forward and tucked my head into his shoulder, my nose pressed against his neck. He wrapped his arms around me and held me to his chest. I breathed in his clean, masculine scent, and tried to commit it to memory. For as long as I lived, I knew I'd never forget him. He was branded on my heart, permanently changing the surface of me, of how my life would go after this.

"Long distance relationships aren't meant to stay that way permanently. And, Jasper, I can't let you give up your dream for me. I won't. We sat in that hotel room together, and you painted this beautiful picture of all the places you wanted to go in New Zealand, and how much of the world there was left for you to see. How you wanted to build things, create things that benefited the people who lived there. Now here we are, with you on the cusp of that, and you want me to tell you not to go. But I can't. I can't love you and take that dream from you." My voice was surprisingly steady, and in the back of my mind I was proud of myself for holding it together for him.

"There has to be a way, Daphne."

"You said, 'What if I don't go,' but that's the wrong question to ask. What if you don't go, and then regret it? What if you don't go, and your opportunity is gone. They give it to someone else, and you never get a second chance. What if you don't go, and you resent me for stopping you? What if I'm the one holding you back from where you're truly supposed to be, and you decide I'm not worth it?" Pain sliced me at the words, but they were true. I couldn't keep him here to watch resentment steal the beauty between us. That would be worse than goodbye. Right?

We swung in silence for several more minutes, and I could tell my words had hit home.

"So, that's it, then. You won't change your answer?" he asked, and his voice was so low it blended with the windchimes on Tracy's porch.

"I won't." My resolve began to waiver, hearing the pain in his voice.

"I will never forget you, Daphne. I'm not sure I can do it—go off and leave you. I've got suitcases in my car, a boarding pass on my phone waiting to be scanned, and yet . . . I don't want to go. I want to stay here with you held against my chest, and chain myself to your swing until something changes." He paused, and for a few minutes we just swung together. Back and forth, staring at nothing and holding onto the precious moment.

An alarm beeped on his phone, and his sigh ruffled my hair. Dread pooled in my stomach because I knew what that meant. It was time.

Leaning away from his safe, warm chest felt like riding your bike up the biggest hill in town as a little kid. Your whole body strained with the effort, sweat broke out on your forehead, and you just weren't sure you'd make it before you slid back down, no matter how hard you pushed those pedals. He was gravity—oxygen—and I was a drowning woman in his absence.

Before I could get too far away from him, he swooped in and caught me. His hands went into my hair, and he leaned in lightning quick and planted his lips on mine. The sudden intensity took the breath right out of my chest. His kiss started out fierce, possessive, but gradually lightened to pure sweetness. So much emotion, so many feelings that couldn't be expressed through words, we both poured into that kiss.

I was dazed when he pulled away, and my eyes fluttered down to lock on his lips. I wanted them back, I wanted to kiss him again, I wanted to chain him to me, forget the porch swing. But instead, he stood. He let his fingertips trail down my cheek as softly as a whisper one more time, and then he turned and walked away.

I watched him climb into his car, back from my driveway, and pull away down my road. Then, when he was beyond my sight, the dam burst.

Fifteen

Empty

Three days later

Rain pounded the window, and Barc's whine pulled me from the endless reruns of "America's Next Top Model" on the TV. "Do you want to go outside, Barc?" I asked, and he lifted a paw to scratch the door in response.

"Okay, I'm coming." I peeled my cheek from the couch pillow and shuffled to the back door. He streaked past me as soon as it slid open, out into the rain. He must have really had to go, because usually he hated getting his paws wet.

I leaned my forehead against the glass of the door, not bothering to sit back down. He'd be back quickly, since he hated the rain. No need to get up twice.

My mind floated, numb after so many days of pain and sadness. Pain was truly inadequate for how I felt watching Jasper leave me. Anguish, suffering, and regret were the tip of the iceberg. The fact that it was the right thing for him eased the pain, barely.

Barc whined at the other side of the door, and I robotically slid it open for him to enter again. My phone buzzed from the couch, so I grabbed it as I sank back into my pillow nest, and paused Tyra mid-sentence.

"Hey, Bea, what's up?"

"What's up with you? I just went by the travel agency, and Carole Leigh was there instead of you."

"Oh, yeah, she's my fill-in when I'm out." I rolled onto my back, and stared up at the ceiling.

"I know that, the question is more along the lines of, why are you still out? It's Tuesday, and we've been back since Saturday."

"It's Tuesday? Huh." I paused, surprised but still not caring. The days were running together. "Well, I've just got the travel crud. You know, you go on a trip, ride in an airplane with all the circulated air, get somebody's sniffles. I could come in, but I thought it would be better to rest and keep my germs at home." I crossed my fingers behind my back to offset the fib. That still worked as an adult, right?

"Funny, you don't sound sniffly. Is it maybe a different kind of sickness that's gotten hold of you? Lovesickness, perhaps?"

I gritted my teeth at her very inconvenient perception. "Bea . . . I'm fine." Okay, so, finger crossing definitely wouldn't offset that whopper.

"Oh, good, then you'll be ready for movie night. How does Thursday sound? I'm off Friday. We'll make a night of it. Sappy movie. Nail polish. Face masks, the whole nine."

I wanted to reject the offer and keep wallowing, alone with Barc, my couch pillows, and Tyra on loop. However, I knew she'd just show up anyways.

"Movie night is good. One condition, though—no sappy movie. Let's watch an action flick."

"Deal. What do you want to see? Don't say Batman."

That brought a small smile to my lips. "Batman."

"Ugh, why is it always Batman? The joker creeps me out. How many times are you going to make me watch those movies?"

"That's the deal, lady. You want movie night, we're watching Batman. It never gets old."

"I'm going to have nightmares. You're going to have to rock me back to sleep and pet my hair. You know, I think there's going to be a new Batman. Did you hear about that?"

"They can make as many new movies as they want, they won't get any better Batman. Christian Bale is a god among men."

"Eh, maybe. Heath Ledger was so attractive. Why did they have to put all that creepy stuff on his face? Ugh. Leave it to the movies to ruin a good thing. Remember the Eragon movie? Aw-ful!"

I snorted at her ridiculousness. "See you then, Bea."

"See you then."

Friday dawned, and I finally dragged myself out of my house to go to work. Bea, George, my mother, and my father had all called—worried—the day before, ruining the mood, anyways. They meant well, but sometimes you just needed to lock yourself away, not put on a bra, and eat all of the ice cream bars in your freezer over a long weekend. It was good for the soul.

The rain hadn't quit, so the weather was really matching my own personal vibe of, "not here for happiness today," and I appreciated that. I stepped out of Bert's toasty cab and directly into a pot-hole-turned-puddle, soaking halfway up my loafer.

Cursing in my head, I stomped into the office. I should have just stayed at home, cuddled up with Barc. He hadn't soaked my feet since he was a floppy-eared baby. With a resigned sigh, I flipped the door sign to "Open" and squelched my way to the desk.

Welcome back to reality.

I filtered through dozens of emails while waiting for my first appointment of the day to come in. Some were junk, a bunch were automated lead notifications, and the rest were all questions and updates to current itineraries which I'd need to work on and reply back to as soon as possible. I marked all of those so I could try to get through them by the end of the day, and had just finished the first update when the over-the-door bell chimed.

I looked up and spotted Marlie, grin as wide as the state of Texas. "Daphne!! Look at you, girl—you've got that just-vacationed glow! How was your trip? I heard George proposed to Bea on the beach the last night—so romantic."

I mustered up a half-hearted smile for her, but it felt like wrestling an angry pit bull. "Oh, yeah. The setting was perfect." Not at all perfect for finding out your almost-boyfriend is in fact leaving you behind and breaking things off. "Those two were meant to be!"

"Oh, they totally were. Anyone with eyes could see they were moon-eyed for years. I'm glad they finally noticed. What about you? You and Jasper seemed like there might have been a little something-something brewing between you. Is he coming back from his work trip soon?"

A lump rose in my throat, and for a minute I couldn't speak at all. Clearing it, I finally said, "No, actually. He got reassigned to New Zealand. His dream job."

"Well, that royally sucks," Marlie muttered. "I mean, don't get me wrong, that's great about his dream job. But how is he supposed to sweep you off your feet from all the way across the world? New Zealand isn't exactly a hop-skip away."

"No, it isn't. It's okay—we parted on friendly terms. I wish him all the best. What can I do for you this morning? Do you need to change something or book another activity for your trip?"

"Oh, no, girl! I was just coming by to drop the last payment. Tucker got a big bonus at work, so we're paying the trip off early." Her smile was genuine as she passed me the bank envelope, but she searched my eyes as if she could tell something was off. "Are you really okay with him going, Daphne? It's okay not to be okay, you know?"

I looked down at my lap, unsure what to say. I hated to lie, but I also hated to be the pathetic girl moping about someone who was barely a boyfriend. Even if I'd felt so much in such a short time, nobody else knew that. "I will be okay, and that's what matters." I pumped my words with as much confidence as I could, because eventually I would be okay. It wouldn't be today, or maybe even next week, but such was life.

"Amen, girlfriend. Just don't be too hard on yourself, and I'm here if you need someone to talk to."

"I appreciate that, Marlie. You're good people."

"So are you. I heard you have something up your sleeve with the Judes for next week. Is that right? That restaurant has been straight up sad for a while now."

I shrugged one shoulder. "I just had an idea—they are the ones running with it. I do think it's going to make everybody happy, though."

"Well, the suspense is downright killin' me. I can't wait to see what y'all came up with. Anywho, I'll let you get back at it. I'm sure you've got a lot of catching up to do . . . being sick and all." She winked, and then sashayed out the door.

I groaned and glared at the ceiling briefly. Apparently everybody in this teacup-sized town knew the real source of my "illness." Dadgum gossips, every last one.

I made it the rest of week without incident, other than a few more nosey townsfolk swinging by to tell me they hoped I was feeling better, and even one or two prying to find out the secret for next week's reveal at Jude's. I was tight-lipped on both counts, so none of them stayed too long, thank the good Lord. Now, I sat and tried to force myself to pay close attention to Mrs. Murphy, as she described her dream cruise. It sounded lovely, but I could plan a kick-butt cruise in roughly twelve minutes, and she'd been going on for . . . my gaze wandered to the clock . . . seventy-eight minutes. Her appointment had only been scheduled for forty-five, but given she was my last client of the day I didn't cut her off. She was very enthusiastic, if a bit repetitive.

My head was starting to pound, though, so I tried to gently steer the conversation to a close. "That sounds lovely, Mrs. Murphy, and I think you've given me plenty to go on. Why don't I put together a few different package options and have you and Mr. Murphy back in for a slideshow, say, next week. How does Thursday at lunch sound to you?" I spun to my computer, and pulled up my calendar.

"Well, are you quite sure, dear? I really want to make sure we take the best possible advantage. It is our forty-fourth anniversary. I want it to be as perfect as it can be. I am happy to stay right here and work through all the fine details with you."

"Yes, ma'am, I will make sure it's unforgettable, I promise. The slideshow is really the best, because then you can see all those options, instead of just reading about them. After that, we can take our time going through each detail." I made a begrudging mental note to schedule two hours for that appointment.

"All right, then. I guess I'll be going." She patted her hair to make sure everything was in place before gathering her handbag and leaving the office. She was one foot out the door when she turned and fired her parting shot. "Just remember, unforgettable could mean it's terrible, and we don't want that."

It was with great relief that I flipped the door sign to "Closed" on a long exhale. Then, I sneezed. My head really was pounding, and my throat felt a bit scratchy from all the talking today. By the time Bert delivered me to my driveway, all I could think about was crawling my shivering self into my bed, and burying myself under the covers. The sneezes had grown in intensity, and congestion had set in with shocking speed.

I let Barc out, filled his bowl for the night, and collapsed face-first into my bed. After toeing my shoes off the side, I curled up and went right to sleep.

The insistent buzzing of my phone in my back pocket woke me an hour later. I fumbled for it, and held it to my ear still, half-asleep and muzzy.

"Hello?"

"Daphne, hey. Are we still on for girl's night? You didn't respond to any of my texts about the pizza, or if you wanted a coconut mask or a clay one. You sound kind of awful, though. Is everything okay?"

As my head cleared, I took stock of myself and realized I was not, in fact, all right. "I think I need to reschedule girls' night. Remember the cold I said I had Tuesday?"

"Yes, the imaginary one."

"Well, it decided to show up for real," I grumbled.

"That sucks. Can I bring you anything? Soup? Still want pizza?" she offered helpfully.

"No, I'm just going to go to bed early, and hope for relief."

"Okay, well, if that changes, you know where to find me."

"Thanks, Bea. Tell George I said hi." I knew she'd visit him tonight instead, since I canceled on her. After I hung up and let Barc—who'd been gleefully rolling in something in the backyard, nonplussed by his extended play time—back in, I took the hottest shower I could stand for the steam, and then crawled back under the covers.

Two minutes later, I was out.

The next morning, someone knocked on the front door while I was puttering in the kitchen, waiting for my coffee maker to bless me with its sweet elixir. Barc raced off, nails clacking down the hall as he broke land speed records to check out our visitor. When I finally made my way after him and opened the door, I was surprised to find George on the other side.

"Can I come in?"

"You can, but I don't recommend it. There's a nine-ty-seven percent chance I have the plague, and you might get it."

He snorted and stepped in the door without comment.

"Okay, but don't say I didn't warn you." I shut the door behind him, and we walked back to the living room.

"I brought you soup from Mom, and your favorite crusty bread from the bakery. Mom and Celia both send their love."

I sniffed the container he handed me, and the scents of warm herbs and chicken greeted me. "That was really sweet of you, and them. Want a cup of coffee? It's almost ready."

"I'll get it, you sit down." He took back the food and walked to the kitchen, but tossed over his shoulder on the way, "Then we're going to talk."

Oh brother.

He came back sporting two mugs of steaming coffee, and passed me one. "Cream and extra sugar, just how you like it."

"Thanks, George."

"Welcome. Now, how are you doing? I know you're sick, but are you upset about something?" He paused, tugging at the collar of his shirt as if it bothered him. "Is it because I didn't tell you before I proposed to Bea? I honestly thought you'd be happy, and I didn't want you to have to keep anything from her if I told you in advance. If that hurt you, I apologize." His face was etched with concern, and the sincere concern in his eyes brought a tear to mine. Dang brothers, making you cry before coffee.

I was floored by the completely unnecessary apology. "No, George. I'm not upset about that at all, I'm just happy for you both. Honestly, you two are perfect together."

He sagged with relief, but then confusion dragged his eyebrows together. "Are you still upset about Jasper? I didn't think you two were that close . . . What happened?"

Remembering the cup in my hand, I delayed answering by taking a sip. "At the moment, I'm sick. But, yes, earlier it was about Jasper. As for what happened—well, he left." I shrugged, not sure what else to say.

He leaned back into the couch cushions, contemplative as he also sipped his coffee. Seeming to make a decision, he spoke again. "Well, I just spoke to him yesterday. He's made it to New Zealand, and he has already started the new job." He stopped, not saying anything else for a minute.

Forcing a neutral tone, I said, "Good, I'm glad he's happy. I wish him all the best over there." I really did want him to be happy, even if I was agonizing over his absence. He was too good a person to wish anything else for, no matter what my selfish heart wanted.

"That's just the thing, Daphne. He's not happy. You're miserable, skipping out on work. He's miserable, throwing himself into work he doesn't sound excited about, even though it's a huge opportunity. I didn't put that together before, but it makes a heck of a lot more sense now. Are you sure this is the best thing, for both of you? Because I'm not."

His frank assessment surprised me, but it shouldn't. George was as straightforward as they came. "It wasn't my decision, George. He got a job offer; he had to go. His job is constantly moving, so nothing between us was going to be permanent. Why am I even explaining this? He contracted for your company—you already know it was temporary." I ran a hand through my unbrushed hair, frustrated with the situation.

"Huh. But if he wasn't, you'd be, what, dating?" He eyed me with speculation.

I groaned. "I don't know, George. We'd be . . . something. We'd only just started getting closer, and he got that call, and . . . that was that." I threw my hands up in exasperation.

"But you've never dated more than casually, so this is different. You actually cared—" He trailed off, speaking to himself more than me at this point. He grimaced, finally catching up. "I'm sorry, Daphne. I can only imagine how I'd feel if Bea up and left."

I swallowed, prepping to tell him that it wasn't the same, that he and Bea were engaged, and Jasper and I weren't that serious . . . but I couldn't. Because Jasper was the first—and only—man I'd ever seen the possibility of more with. God, that stung.

Realizing he was waiting for a response, I floundered for something, and ended up shrugging. "It is what it is. We don't always get what we want. I'll be okay."

He looked sad, and the expression somehow amplified my own sadness. George was perpetually happy and upbeat, so the sadness was ill-fitting on him.

"I know you will—you're as tough as they come. All your medical issues over the years, going through that at such a young age . . . pretty sure you're stronger than I am in all the ways that count."

I smiled at that. "Don't you forget it."

He shook his head at my bravado, his familiar smile back in place. "Okay then, I'll let you get back to your rest. If you need anything at all, call me. I'll be your delivery man." He gave me a rib-cracking hug, and then let himself out.

Once again, I was alone with my thoughts. And all I felt was the empty hole where Jasper had just taken root, and been snatched away. I was hollow.

Sixteen

Worth It

The cold passed over the weekend, and my days took on a monotonous tone. Work, care for Barc, watch reruns, and sleep. The week passed in a distracted blur. I was in a funk, and nothing seemed apt to break it right away. I'd rescheduled girls night with Bea for this Saturday, and tonight was the celebratory Jude's dinner. The whole town was buzzing, but I still felt flat. I'd tried to beg off, claiming exhaustion, but Janie Jude wouldn't hear it.

So, after a quick trip home to let Barcelona out, feed him, and give him some good ear scratches, I was heading back to town for the celebration. As I pulled up in front of the familiar old building, the packed parking area brought a smile to my face.

If nothing else, we'd already succeeded in getting people back in here, which was all I cared about. The sweet tea boycott was absolutely ridiculous, and hopefully people would remember what they were missing after tonight.

I climbed out of Bert's cab with a new spring in my step, and more interest than I'd felt in the two weeks since the awful parting with Jasper. No, I am not thinking about him tonight. Tonight, I'm focusing on the good still in my life. I straightened my shoulders and lifted my chin, then pushed through the swinging door. I scanned the packed restaurant for Bea and George, and spotted them across the crowd in a small booth at the very back. I crossed the room, and was stopped a few times by friends and clients.

I even spotted Dolly Blake, clearly ruffled and not happy about the great turnout for the Judes. She wasn't outright glaring, but her smile was as fake as a two-dollar spray tan.

"Hey, guys," I said as I slid into my side of the booth.

"Hey, Daphne! This is sooo exciting!" Bea was practically bouncing in her seat. "I can't believe you haven't told me what's going on. That's definitely breaking some sort of best friend law."

I snorted. "It wasn't mine to tell. It's finally time, so calm yourself."

George gave me a warm smile, and then Janie and Beau Jude walked to the back of the restaurant where the big "Specials" chalkboard was covered with a red cloth.

Janie's smile was wide as Beau spoke to the crowd, "Hey, y'all, we really appreciate you coming out tonight. Your support means a lot."

There was a smattering of applause, but it died down quickly.

"We wanted to try something different, to keep things fresh. We know that wasn't super popular."

A grumbling rose around the room, but he gestured for quiet and people settled. "However, with a little help, I think we've figured out a way to keep the traditional favorites as they should be, and still bring new, exciting things to our beautiful little town. With that being said, Granny's classic sweet tea is back to its former, unchanged glory."

Cheers rose around the room, and I looked over to see Dolly smiling smugly while she clapped. She issued sanctimonious nods to anyone she made eye contact with, as if she was personally responsible for the decision.

"We also have something completely new for you all." He looked over at Janie, and she crossed to the other side of the board and grabbed the red cover. With a nod, they both pulled it down to reveal the new specials board. Some of it was the usual—Sunday roast with gravy and veggies, and Friday night fish fry. But there, at the bottom, was a new set of drink specials—The Island Peach Breeze, and Frosted Island Peach were chalked in under a palm tree with bright colors and extra flourishes.

"To celebrate, we've got samples for everyone." Everyone cheered again as the wait staff started circulating with trays full of miniature cups, sporting the pale peach drinks. Speech accomplished, the Judes circulated through the room, stopping and talking at every table.

"Okay, so what is this Island Peach Breeze, exactly?" George asked.

"Well, while I was holed up with my sunburn, Jasper brought me another soursop juice. We were talking about how we'd miss it when we went home, and an idea struck me. What if we could make it with something closer to home? So, I asked the front desk if they would pretty please part with a recipe. It took some wheedling, but they actually did give it to me in the end. So, I brought it to the Judes, they loved it, and have been working on incorporating fresh peaches for a Georgia spin. They perfected a new recipe, and here we are."

A waitress reached our table, and we all took long swigs from the samples she passed out.

"Ho-ly cow. This is flipping amazing!" Bea chugged hers in no time, and stole sips of George's.

It really was delicious, with a hint of the original soursop, but with a rich thread of peaches blended in. They'd let me try a few different variations last week, but we'd all agreed this recipe was the best. When our waitress came back, we ordered chicken pot pies all around, with another round of Island Peach Breezes.

A couple hours later, everyone was stuffed to the gills but reluctant to leave now that they were back in the familiar welcoming dining room of Jude's. I even felt a little lighter, glad that I had a small hand in bringing the town back together, as we should have been all along.

Bea was laughing at something George said, when a murmur started up on the other side of the dining room. I turned to see what was going on—surely not trouble again that fast—but what I saw stopped my heart mid-beat. There, standing just inside the doorway, looking exhausted and somewhat worse for the wear, was Jasper. He was still as a statue—except his eyes, which scanned each table, looking for someone. I half-rose from the table, unable to stop myself. The motion caught his attention, and our eyes locked. Determination stole over him, and he started towards me. I stood, and met him in the aisle.

"Jasper? What are you doing here? You're supposed to be in New Zealand." I looked down and took in his rumpled clothes, and then back up at his mussed hair and the tired lines on his face. He looked like he'd just climbed out of a plane.

"You're wrong. I'm not supposed to be in New Zealand." He reached forward with both hands, and clasped mine. "I'm exactly where I'm supposed to be—with you."

"I—"

"No," he cut me off, "let me finish. I know that you think things have to carry on as they are, but they don't. Yes, I've traveled for work; yes, New Zealand was my dream. But that doesn't mean it's where I'm supposed to be now."

"Was your dream?" My mind had latched onto that tiny discrepancy, hope starting to blossom, despite my efforts to squash it down.

"Was. You are my dream, Daphne. The time I've spent with you has meant more than any trip I've ever been on. New Zealand was beautiful, and the people were great, and I spent a week and a half consulting on an amazing project with brilliant people. I should have been ecstatic, but instead all I felt was flat. Because I was alone. Did you know, that never bothered me before? But now, all I could think about was what you'd think of New Zealand, what you'd think of the project. How you'd love something one of the locals said about an obscure bit of history. When I'd turn around and you weren't there, it was all wrong." He drew in a ragged breath.

"But Jasper, it's your job. There's nothing here for you . . ." He raised a finger to my lips, stopping me again.

"It's not my job anymore. I quit."

My mouth dropped open, and I was speechless.

"You asked me before, what if I didn't go, and later resented you for missing the opportunity. But that wasn't the right question. The question was, what if I went and hated it? What if I went, and instead of loving the beautiful, rolling hills, I just missed your beautiful, kind face? What if no location in the world means as much to me as this woman, in this place. What if we put down roots together? What if we built a life right here, right where we're meant to be? What if you're it for me, and my biggest regret in life would be leaving you behind? That is the question you should be asking." He ran a finger along my jawline, and I couldn't stop the shudder that rolled through me.

Was this really happening? Had he really come back for me, quit his job for me?

"Jasper, I don't know what to say. I'm so glad that you're here, I don't even have words." I tried desperately to hold back the tears building behind my eyes. He was so eloquent, and I was going to dissolve into a puddle in a moment. All the heartache and pain the last two weeks had built, and demanded release now that he was here in front of me again.

"Maybe we don't need words," he whispered, and then swooped forward and claimed my lips in a kiss that I'd never forget. Heat blossomed in my belly and burned through my veins. My heart was pounding so hard in my chest, it felt like it was trying to escape. I was so consumed by his kiss that I barely heard the cheer that went up around the whole restaurant. I reached up and twined my fingers into his soft hair—claiming him right back—and in that moment I knew I wasn't letting him go again. I'd done what I thought was best before, but if the last two weeks of pain and wanting him had taught me anything, it was that I didn't have a freaking clue what was best. I just knew that it was time to follow my heart—and it was screaming that I needed this man in my life.

When we eventually parted, all I could do was stare into his eyes and grin like an absolute fool.

George's jovial voice broke through the love-induced haze I was in.

"Hey, man, why don't you sit down. Stay a while."

Jasper linked his fingers with mine, never breaking eye contact. "I think I'll do just that."

SEVENTEEN

Epilogue

SIX MONTHS LATER

"**M**y apartment is perfectly adequate for two people. You can just move in with me after the wedding," Bea insisted.

"Adequate is the key word. I know you're comfortable there, but I have a whole house. Why would we go to a one-bedroom apartment, when we could have a whole house?" George argued.

"Because your house is already occupied by a second person who is not me. There's no reason to make Finn move out, when I have a perfectly good apartment and a lease that doesn't end for eight more months."

"Right, but we're going to be married soon, and it doesn't make sense to move twice. We should start off where we want to stay, and it's more logical to go with more space."

I chomped a massive bite from the side of my chocolate cinnamon donut, and watched the conversation volley back and forth like a tennis match. These two were an even match, and I had a feeling we'd be here for a while. I scooched back from the dainty table, and walked over to where Celia was pretending to wipe the spotless counter so she could keep an eye on the soon-to-be newlyweds. Six weeks until the big day, and they still had some decisions to make.

"Can I get another coffee, Celia? I need the caffeine to keep up with them."

"Sure thing, sugar." She gave me a motherly smile, and then retreated to the coffee maker to freshen up my cup. I'd only come by this morning to hammer out the last few honeymoon details, but once the wedding discussions had started, it was a runaway train that I couldn't stop. I'd already sent messages postponing all of my clients before noon. Hopefully by then we'd have made some headway.

A chime from the door drew my attention, and I smiled with genuine pleasure at the unexpected appearance of my main squeeze, Jasper.

"Jasper! What are you doing here?" I lowered my voice and pointed feverishly at our table with my thumb. "Run while you still can. Wedding central will suck you in too, if you let it."

He chuckled, but didn't take my warning and bolt. Instead, he greeted Celia when she handed me my coffee, and ordered one of his own.

"I'm just in for a morning cuppa. A little birdie told me you'd be here, so I had to stop before I went to the job site. Twelve hours is far too long to go without seeing you." He dropped a kiss on my cheek, and I smiled warmly at him. For some guys, that might have been a disingenuous comment, but not for Jasper. Ever since he'd come back, we spent time together every day, even if it was only on the phone when one of us had an unavoidably long day at work.

"How is that new project coming along?" I asked, sipping my coffee.

"Oh, fine. They sent over some additional changes, so I'll be hammering those out today, but after that we get to move on to the next phase."

"That sounds fancy, which is ironic because the next phase is usually when all the construction workers get started, right?" He nodded. "Well, I can't wait to see this one when it's done. The drawings you showed me were gorgeous."

"What can I say, I've been feeling particularly inspired lately." He nudged me with his elbow right as his phone rang. Passing me his cup, he pulled it from his pocket. His mom's smiling face showed on the screen.

"Ooh, let me have it." Without waiting for permission, I nabbed the phone and answered the video call. "Good morning, Agnes!" I sang.

"Daphne! Oh, it's so nice to see you again! What are you two doing, canoodling at this hour? Shouldn't you both be at work?" I laughed at her instant switch to mom-mode.

"No canoodling, just ran into a handsome fella over coffee, and decided to steal his phone." I waved the cup at her, and shifted the phone so she could see Jasper over my shoulder as well. "Besides, I am working. George and Bea are finalizing honeymoon details today, so I met them at the bakery. Which, I might add, you still haven't come to visit yet. I am disappointed!" I pouted, knowing she'd get a kick out of my insistence that she come visit in person. It was our bit.

"Well, for the first time, you're in luck! I've called to say your father and I are coming down next month. We'll need you to arrange a place for us to stay. Are there any good B&Bs there? Hotels are nice, but B&Bs always have better pets."

I chuckled at that, but she wasn't wrong. And I was finally going to get to meet her! "I'm sure we can find you a place with an excellent house pet. If not, though, Barc is sure to drown you in kisses."

"Yes, I can't wait to meet my grand-dog. I will be bringing treats for him."

"Mum, you can't seriously intend to pack dog biscuits with you," Jasper leaned over my shoulder to interject.

She set her chin, and gave him a stern look. "I can and will. I'll not hear another word from you on the subject, if you know what's good for you."

"Yes, Mum. I'll just be happy to see you and Dad."

"We're excited too! I'll send you the dates, but I've got to run for now. You two have a good day, now!" She waved, and hung up before we could respond. She was a trip, and I loved her to pieces. Almost as much as I loved her delightful son.

I passed his phone back, and he tucked it away again. "Unfortunately, I do need to get going." He sat the coffee cup down, and threaded his hands around my waist to wrap me in a hug. "I'm already counting down the minutes until I get to see you tonight."

I pressed a kiss to his cheek, and hugged him back. I was reluctant to let him go, but it would only be a few hours before date night. "Knock 'em dead at work today." I pretend-punched him on the shoulder, and he shook his head at my antics.

After he'd gone, Celia commented from her spot against the back counter, "You've picked a good one, Daphne. He's a real keeper."

"Somehow, I think you knew that from the beginning." I raised one eyebrow in speculation.

She just gave me a bemused smile, and let me think what I wanted.

I walked back to the table, and sat down. Bea and George hadn't missed a beat, and were still debating the housing situation.

"But why should we pay extra for parking a second vehicle, when parking at my house is free?" George asked.

"That is true, but—"

Having had enough of this particular line of conversation, I decided to stick my nose in. "Hey, I've got an idea. Why don't you do a swap. You two move into George's house, but see if Finn wants to take over the last few months of your lease. Easy-peasy."

They both paused, and exchanged a long look. George spoke first—"That . . . could work. I can ask him, if you're okay with the idea."

Bea shrugged. "It's the best idea we've got for now, and I'd feel better if he had somewhere to go immediately."

Satisfied with that, they moved on to debating which groom's cake flavor they wanted, and I once again let my mind wander. Wedding planning wasn't my bag, but I was happy for them.

Another chime at the door caught my attention a few minutes later.

A gorgeous olive-skinned woman with a head full of shining black curls stood just inside the door, hesitant. Celia noticed her immediately, and came from behind the counter.

"Maggie? What in the world are you doing here!? I wasn't expecting you—is everything all right?" She sounded concerned, and pulled her into a firm hug.

"Hey, Aunt Celia. No, you weren't expecting me. Uhm . . ." She pushed some of her wild curls back behind her ear, where they immediately sprang free. "Josie and I needed a change of scenery." She blew out a breath, and squared her shoulders. "Richie left, and I was wondering if we could stay with you for a while?"

Celia's look turned fierce in an instant, and she held Maggie by the upper arms. "You don't even have to ask—you always have a place here with me in Adele. Now, where is our sweet girl?"

My eyes drifted down, and I spotted the adorable little girl clinging to the back of Maggie's purse. She couldn't have been more than five or six, and she looked sad. Her serious little expression cracked my heart right in two.

Celia scooped her up, and carted her straight to the pastry case, where she started pointing to all of the many dainty options displayed there. Maggie sagged back against the door frame, looking deflated and weary now that her daughter was in someone else's care.

I stood and crossed the floor, and stuck my hand out for her to shake. "Hi, Maggie, I'm Daphne. Welcome to Adele."

Hey, y'all! I'm so glad you read Will Travel for Love! I hope you enjoyed reading it as much as I enjoyed writing it. Adele, Georgia is my happy place. If so, and you'd consider leaving a review (or just dropping some stars, if you're not sure what to say!) I'd be over the moon. Reviews are GOLD for new authors. Now, if you've got your sweet tea ready and a comfy chair, book three, Waiting on Forever, is ready for you!

Maggie is a soon-to-be divorcée with a six-year-old daughter looking up to her every step of the way. She's doing her best to navigate her new circumstances with grace, but we all know how hard that can be, especially when matters of the heart are involved. Will she give Jensen a chance to prove he's different than her ex, or will she shut him out before he's ever had a chance?

Read Waiting on Forever now!

Before You Go . . .

Thank you so much for reading Will Travel for Love! I do hope you enjoyed it, and are looking forward to the next book in the series as much as I enjoyed writing it. As a new author, your review means the world to me. If you would take a moment to leave a rating or review before you go on to your next read, I would be over the moon to see it.

If you'd like to sign up for my mailing list so you never miss a new release, and get fun freebies from time to time like recipes, short stories, and more, you can do so here (subscribepage.com/KristenDi xon)!

I am available by email at kristendixonauthor@g mail.com as well, if you'd ever like to drop me a line directly!

Also By Kristen Dixon

Bless Your Heart (FREE!!!!!)
Thirty and unmarried in the south, can Marlie find
her forever wedding date? A romantic short story
sure to make you smile.

Bea Mine (Sweet Nothings Bake Shop, Book 1)
**The quirky baker. Her best friend's off-limits older
brother. When sparks—and frosting—fly between
them, it'll be a Valentine's Day to remember.**
When two stubborn southerners don't see eye to
eye, it's bound to cause sparks. But if these two can't

see heart to heart, it might just be the worst mistake the small town of Adele, Georgia has ever seen. This clean contemporary novella will have you falling in love from the first chapter.

Will Travel for Love (Sweet Nothings Bake Shop, Book 2)
A small town girl. An alluring British engineer who's just passing through. Will she follow her head, or lose her heart?
Check out book two of the Sweet Nothings Bake Shop series, and see what Celia's got up her sleeve for Daphne. Or should we say, who she's got up her sleeve?

Waiting on Forever (Sweet Nothings Bake Shop, Book 3)
She's healing from the blindside of divorce. He's a small-town hero. Can they build something together, or will it all fall apart?
With the two of them at odds, tension builds in the most unlikely of ways. Will her stubborn pride keep her lonely forever, or will Jensen be able to prove he's got enough heart to share with Maggie and her daughter?

The Bachelor Bargain (Sweet Nothings Bake Shop, Book 4)

An outspoken graphic designer. The town's most introverted bachelor. Will they open up to each other, or will the town's zany attempts at matchmaking push them further apart?

One sunset dinner won't change a thing . . . until it changes *everything*.

The Ferguson Brothers Series (coming 2023)

About the Author

Kristen Dixon was born and raised in Jacksonville, Florida, and is happily married with two kids. She has worked as a restaurant hostess, library book shelver, ranch hand, trail riding guide, and about twelve other unrelated fields, because variety—and sweet tea—is the spice of life. Not to mention a little thing called pursuing her passion of writing. She likes to write late in the evenings and thinks baking great cookies fuels hopes and dreams.

Her books are sweet, clean, and southern with real heart. If you like a classic southern gentleman, quirky side characters, and small towns, well, y'all came to the right place. Grab some tea, pull up a chair, and get ready to sit a spell.

If you would like to get all the latest news about her works, you can sign up for her newsletter at h ttps://www.subscribepage.com/KristenDixon and as always, don't forget to Follow on Amazon!

www.ingramcontent.com/pod-product-compliance
Lightning Source LLC
Chambersburg PA
CBHW050419260626
47156CB00003B/1072